This book should be returned to any branch of the
Lancashire County Library on or before the date shown

- 2 FEB 2019

2 4 JUL 2019

2 8 AUG 2019

D0334737

Lancashire County Library,
County Hall Complex,
1st floor Christ Church Precinct,
Preston, PR1 8XJ

www.lancashire.gov.uk/libraries

LL1(A)

For Cal Carver
~ Barry Hutchison

To Dan (Muesli Pocket)
~ Katie Abey

STRIPES PUBLISHING
An imprint of the Little Tiger Group
1 Coda Studios, 189 Munster Road,
London SW6 6AW

A paperback original
First published in Great Britain in 2018

ISBN: 978-1-84715-906-9

A CIP catalogue record for this book is available
from the British Library.

Printed and bound in the UK.

10 9 8 7 6 5 4 3 2 1

BEAKY MALONE

WEIRDEST SHOW ON EARTH

BARRY HUTCHISON

ILLUSTRATED BY KATIE ABEY

stripes

CHAPTER 1

CASTING CALL

"I'm talking to Leon tonight," I said, plodding along the corridor with my best mate, Theo.

He nodded for quite a long time. "Oh."

"You've forgotten who Leon is, haven't you?"

"Yeah," Theo admitted. "Who is he?"

"The Aberdeen guy," I said. "The one who emailed me about Madame Shirley."

"Oh, him. Cool. Keep me posted," said Theo.

Leon's message had come out of the blue a couple of days before. He said he'd been reading my blog about everything that had happened since my life-changing experience in Madame Shirley's truth-telling machine, and that he was one of her victims, too.

"What do you reckon you're going to be doing in the play?" Theo asked, changing the subject.

I shrugged. "Dunno."

Putting my name down for the Year Seven school play had seemed like a good idea at the time. I thought it'd mean I could skip a few classes, muck around a bit, and generally use it as an excuse to a) do less work, and b) have a bit of a laugh.

Of course that was before Madame Shirley had robbed me of my ability to lie, throwing my whole life into chaos. There was no saying what would happen if I stepped out on stage in front of a packed audience, but it'd probably be memorable. Just not in a good way.

Still, I was missing the last ten minutes of maths, so that was something.

Theo and I shuffled along the corridors, heading for the hall. He had put his name down for the play, too. Or, being honest, *I* had put his name down for it for a laugh, but now I was relieved to have him with me. I was counting on him to dig me out of any trouble my truth-telling might get me into.

"I'm not acting," he said. "No way. I'll be, I don't know, lighting engineer or something."

"You don't know anything about lighting."

ALAS, POOR YORICK! I DIDN'T KNOW HIM AT ALL.

Theo mimed flicking a switch. "On. Off. What else do you need to know?"

I snorted. "It's a play. I think it'll be a bit more complicated than that."

"Not if I'm in charge it won't," Theo said. "You can have all the lights or no lights. Absolute darkness or brighter than the sun."

"I vote for darkness," I said as we pushed through a set of swing doors. "Anyway, maybe *I* should be the one doing the lighting."

"I thought you liked acting?" Theo said.

He was right – I did like acting, and had it not been for the whole "unable to lie" situation, I might have been looking forward to it. Now, though, I had no idea how it was actually going to work.

"I don't know if I can act," I said.

Theo smirked. "You can't. You're rubbish. I've been trying to tell you for years."

"Hey!" I protested. "That's not what I meant.

8

I mean, I can't lie, right?"

"Really?" said Theo. "You've kept that quiet…"

We both knew that wasn't true. I'd told pretty much everyone in school about my encounter with the mysterious Madame Shirley, her shop, and her truth-telling machine, but Theo was the only one who really believed me. My big sister, Jodie, knew it was true, too, but only because she'd shoved me into the machine in the first place.

"If I can't lie, how can I pretend to be someone else?" I asked. "How can I walk out on stage and say, 'Hello, audience, my name's … Acty McActingface'? That would be a lie."

"It'd also be a terrible play, by the sounds of things," said Theo. "Mind you, Brannan's written this one herself, so I doubt it's going to be Shakespeare, either."

I shuddered. "Hope not. Shakespeare's so *boring*."

"Maybe it'll be a love story," said Theo. I looked

round to find him grinning at me and waggling his eyebrows. "Evie's in the play, too."

"What? No! Is she?"

Theo nodded. "She told me in physics. She seemed *very* excited about it. She totally fancies you."

I wanted to deny it but all the evidence pointed to the very real possibility that Evie Green did, in fact, fancy me. She'd even kissed me after our team had won the Winston and Watson Wagstaffe Cup of Competitive Chummery recently. OK, it was just a peck on the cheek, but still...

"Can you blame her?" I said, trying to laugh my embarrassment away. "I'm *easily* a four out of ten on the looks front. Four-point-five if the lighting's right ... and you ignore my nose."

We turned on to the French corridor, where one of the teachers was shouting at his class in a language we didn't understand. French, probably.

It wasn't until we passed the shouty teacher's door that I noticed Theo was still grinning at me. "What?" I asked.

"So...?" said Theo.

"So what?"

Theo sighed. "So, *Evie.*"

My heart began to race. I knew what was coming next and instinctively reached a hand into my pocket. "What about her?"

"Do you like her?" Theo asked.

"Yes, she's pretty cool," I said, frantically unwrapping a plastic bag in my pocket.

"You know what I mean," said Theo. "Do you *fancy* her?"

Before the truth could blurt itself out, I crammed my Emergency Gobstopper into my mouth. With that in place I could barely breathe, let alone speak. And if I couldn't speak, I couldn't humiliate myself - or anyone else.

At least, that was the theory. The reality was that whenever I put the gobstopper in my mouth I ended up dribbling all down my chin, which was fairly humiliating.

"Suit yourself," said Theo. "But I'm totally taking that as a yes."

When we reached the door to the hall I stopped to spit the gobstopper back into its bag, and shoved it in my pocket.

As we stepped inside, we were met with a one-woman standing ovation. "There they are! Our final players have arrived!" crowed Ms Brannan, leaping up from her Director's chair, her rainbow-coloured scarf flapping behind her.

"Romeo, Romeo, wherefore art thou, Romeo?" she said, pointing right in my face. "Oh, look! Found him!"

She laughed like a startled horse, winked at Theo, then gestured up to the stage where a dozen or so other kids were waiting. Evie smiled at me and waved. I nodded and waved back, but only briefly, because I spotted Theo smirking at me from the corner of my eye.

"Wait, 'Romeo'?" I said.

"Yes! We're doing *Romeo and Juliet*!" announced the drama teacher, her eyes enormous behind the lenses of her chunky red glasses.

"Theo said you'd written the play," I said.

"He's right, I did!"

I think I actually heard Theo frown behind me. "What? You wrote *Romeo and Juliet*?" he said. "I thought it was Shakespeare."

Ms Brannan let out another braying laugh. "Quite so, quite so, he did!" she agreed. "But I've brought it bang up to date."

"Oh," said Theo.

"And then continued well beyond the current date and into the distant future!" the teacher explained, pointing towards the end of the hall with a flourish, as if the distant future was somewhere in that direction. "It's *Romeo and Juliet* ... but with aliens!"

"Riiiight," I said. "OK. And what are you calling it?"

"*Romeo and Juliet ... But With Aliens!*" Ms Brannan announced.

Theo puffed out his cheeks. "Well, it's certainly descriptive."

"Does what it says on the tin," I agreed.

"I'm glad you approve," the teacher said.

She spun on the spot and gestured grandly at the gathered Year Sevens. I knew most of them – Evie, obviously, plus her friend, Chloe, who was currently pouting at her phone. Wayne, my former arch-nemesis, was there, too, probably so he could get close to Chloe.

NAME: WAYNE
ROLE: BULLY
LOVES: CHLOE
HATES: BEAKY

NAME: EVIE
ROLE: LOVE INTEREST
LOVES: BEAKY
FRIEND: CHLOE

NAME: CHLOE
ROLE: POPULAR GIRL
LOVES: HERSELF
FRIEND: EVIE

NAME: DUNCAN
ROLE: NEW BOY
LOVES: EVERYTHING
HATES: WAYNE

Duncan, the tiny new boy, was standing at the side of the group, keeping a safe distance from Wayne, and between them stood eight or nine other kids who weren't really in my social circle. Although, to be fair, my social circle was basically a straight line between me and Theo.

"Friends, Romans, Year Sevens, lend me your ears!" said Ms Brannan. "You have all signed up for this year's 'Play in a Week' scheme, in which we will be producing a brand-new play, before performing it on Friday evening."

She gestured to a pile of scripts on the stage. "I've written something I think is absolutely brilliant, quite frankly, and have assigned everyone a role. Some are theatrical, others technical, but all vitally important to…"

She stopped talking when she realized no one was paying attention. Everyone had grabbed a script and flicked to the first page where all our names were listed.

Sure enough, my name was right at the top.

'Romeonulan: Dylan Malone.'

"Lighting engineer!" said Theo. "Get in."

"Wardrobe assistant?" said Chloe. She wrinkled her nose. "Does that mean, like, costume designer?"

"Not really," said Ms Brannan.

Chloe sniffed and took out a pen. "I'll put 'costume designer'," she said, scribbling on her script.

Beside me Theo gave a snort. "Have you checked out the rest of the cast?" he asked, looking at me and then at his script.

I frowned. "What?" It took me a moment to notice but then my blood ran cold.

'Julietraxis: Evie Green.'

Oh no!

"Stage hand?" said Wayne. "What does that mean?"

Ms Brannan waved vaguely. "It means you'll be building the props, designing the sets. Uh, carrying things. You know? I got the impression you were good with your hands."

"I am," Wayne replied, nodding proudly. He shot Chloe a sideways look. "I once strangled a rat."

Chloe's face contorted in horror. "Ew."

"No," said Wayne, flapping in panic. "By accident, I meant."

"You strangled a rat *by accident*?" I said.

Wayne glared at me. He and I had been arch-enemies for years, but after our recent victory at the Winston and Watson Wagstaffe Cup of Competitive Chummery (or the WAWWCOCC for short) an uneasy truce had developed between us. At least, he hadn't attempted to punch my face

17

through a wall in the past few days, which was about as close to a truce as I was likely to get.

"Yes, Beaky," he hissed. "By accident."

He was saved by Ms Brannan, who announced that she was putting us through some drama warm-ups. This involved running around to various parts of the hall, pulling faces at one another and shouting out random words in funny accents. Most of us joined in, except Chloe, who spent most of the time either looking at her phone or rolling her eyes at us, and Wayne, who stood near Chloe, shaking his head in our general direction.

Once the warm-up was finished, we all got up on stage.

Evie sidled over to me. "Hey, co-star," she said, tucking a loose strand of hair behind her ear and smiling.

"Uh, hi. Hello. Evie. Yes," I fumbled. I smiled awkwardly, caught Theo smirking at me, then pointed to the script. "I don't think I can do it," I said.

"What?" said Ms Brannan, in something not far off a shriek. "Why?"

"It's like I keep telling everyone, I can't lie."

"Not this again," tutted Wayne.

"Even if you couldn't lie, why would that matter?" said Evie, looking puzzled – and a little disappointed. "Why would that stop you being in the play?"

"Well, I'm not Romeo, am I? Or Alien Romeo or whoever. If I *pretend* I am, then I'm lying," I explained. I stopped on a page with one of my lines on it. "I can't just stand up and say, 'Forsooth, I have been trapped in hyper-sleep without food for months,' can I? It's not true."

I blinked. "Wait. Did I just say that?"

Evie nodded. Wayne nodded. Even Theo nodded, although he looked a bit confused.

"Theo! Ask me if I've been in hyper-sleep without food for months," I said.

"What? Why?"

"Just do it!"

"Have you been in hyper-sleep without food for months?" Theo asked.

I tried to say "Yes" but the word refused to budge past my lips. "Yyyyy-no."

It was no use. I couldn't lie. And yet...

"Forsooth, I have been trapped in hyper-sleep without food for months," I said, reading the line again.

"Looks like you can read it just fine," said Ms Brannan.

"I can read it just fine," I mumbled. Then the enormity of it hit me. "I can read a script. *I can read a script!*" I cried. "This changes *everything*!"

CHAPTER 2

THE TELLY PEOPLE

Nothing much really happened in the first rehearsal. The technical people went off to talk about … technical things, while the actors did a group reading of the script. To say it was one of the top-five most embarrassing experiences of my life would be an accurate way to describe it, with Evie and I having to confess our undying love for each other, while a boy called Duggie – who, appropriately enough, was playing a space-dog – *woofed* and *barked* in the background.

WOOF!

When I finally got home, I was barged aside at the gate by my big sister, Jodie, who must have been walking behind me the whole time. Her face was flecked with mud.

"Hey, watch it," I protested as she pushed in front of me.

"Where have you been?" she asked, eyeing me suspiciously.

"I had a bit of drama," I said.

"What do you mean? What happened? Did you get into trouble again?" Her eyes became slits. "Did you get *me* into trouble again?"

"No, I mean I had drama. I'm in the school play."

Jodie tutted. "I thought you meant something happened to you."

"Something *did* happen to me," I said. "I can read a script."

I explained to Jodie about how I'd been able to deliver the lines without any problems. I'd even been able to stand in the middle of the stage and loudly announce, "My name is Romeonulan of Glauxus IV," when clearly that wasn't the case.

"Yeah, but that's not lying, is it?" Jodie said, once I'd finished. "It's acting."

"Same thing," I argued.

"No, it isn't!" said Jodie. "People don't win 'Best Liar' at the Oscars, do they?"

I shoulder-barged her aside and raced to get into the house before her. She lunged for me at the door and, as we both stumbled in, we saw Dad standing behind a xylophone in the middle of the living room. He was wearing his dressing gown, slippers, and a pair of imitation designer sunglasses he'd bought for a pound at the market, and which he – wrongly – thought made him look cool.

Destructo, our dog, was sprawled across the entire length of the couch. As we entered, he raised a head and shot us a long-suffering look that seemed to say, "Run, while you still have the chance."

"There you are!" Dad said. "Where have you been?"

"Drama," I said.

"Hockey practice," said Jodie.

"Right, good," said Dad, vaguely waving the xylophone beaters around. "I need your opinion on something. What do you reckon to this?"

He began gently tapping the same two notes and then broke into song.

"Dogs. Dogs, dogs, dogs,
D-d-d-dogs. Dogs, dogs,
Dogs,
Not cats,
Dogs, dogs, d-dogs,

D-d-dogs,
Dogs!"

He stopped playing, took a bow, then grinned at us. "Well?"

"Well what?" asked Jodie.

"It's my new song," said Dad. "What do you think?"

"What's it about?" I asked.

Dad tutted. "What do you mean, 'What's it about?' It's about dogs, isn't it?"

"I get that," I said. "I just wondered if maybe I was missing something. You know, if there was a deeper meaning or...?" I saw the confused look on Dad's face. "Apparently not. So it's mostly just you saying 'dogs' over and over again, then?"

"While bashing a xylophone," added Jodie.

"It's a work in progress," said Dad tetchily.

Dad's job – although, I use that term loosely – is writing jingles for radio adverts. If you've ever heard a song on the radio about spot cream, sink unblockers or adult nappies, chances are my dad wrote it.

Dad realized he was still wearing his sunglasses and whipped them off. "I reckon that song could make us rich!"

"How?" I asked. "Are you going to get people to pay you to never sing it again?"

"No, I'm going to sell it to the telly people."

Jodie and I exchanged a look. Working from home by himself all day, Dad sometimes goes off on strange flights of fancy that, to the casual observer, could appear to be full-blown insanity. It

was possible he'd convinced himself that not only did little people live inside our TV, but that they were willing to pay him lots of money for a song about dogs.

"What telly people?" Jodie asked, smiling kindly.

"Oh, wait, I should have started with that,

shouldn't I?" said Dad. "We're going to be on the telly! Well, you are, Dylan. You and Destructo."

I frowned. "What? Why?"

"Because Destructo has been chosen for – wait for it – *TV's Most Talented Dogs!*"

My heart stopped and my blood ran cold.

"Do you mean *TV's Most Talented Pets*?" I asked.

Dad blinked. "What? No. It's dogs, isn't it?"

He picked up a letter from the coffee table and read it. Jodie and I both watched him deflate before our eyes. "Argh! It is. It's *pets*. They're never going to want my dog song now. I thought it could be their new theme tune. It feels a bit sort of, I don't know, *racist* to other animals now." He looked thoughtful. "Can animals be racist, do you think?"

"Theo used to have a cat that looked like Hitler," I said, snatching the letter from Dad's hands. "I reckon it was probably a bit racist."

I quickly scanned the letter. "Oh no," I whispered. "Oh no, oh no, oh no."

"What? I thought you'd be happy," said Dad.

"This is a disaster!" I cried, then I raced out into the hall and up the stairs before anyone could quiz me further.

Annoyingly, Jodie decided to follow me.

"Ugh. What's that smell?" she asked, covering her mouth and nose with both hands as she stepped into my room.

"Farts, mostly," I said. I pointed over to the corner. "And that pile of dirty pants and socks."

Jodie visibly recoiled from the mound of washing. It was almost up to my waist, and the only reason Mum hadn't gone mental about it was that she kept mistaking it for a beanbag.

Shaking her head in disgust, Jodie glared at me. "What's the problem?"

"I can't be bothered taking it to the washing machine," I admitted. "And I quite like the smell."

"Ew, you're a freak," she said. "And speaking of

freaks, I meant why the big freak-out over the telly thing?"

The letter from the production company was still clutched in my hand. I looked down at it again. "I entered Destructo into *TV's Most Talented Pets*," I said.

"Why? Destructo hasn't got any talents," said Jodie. "Beyond eating everything and being huge. What did you…?"

Her eyes widened. "Wait. Did you enter him before or after the truth-telling machine?"

I smiled weakly. "Before."

Jodie groaned. "Oh no. And what did you tell them he could do?"

"You've got to understand, I thought it'd be funny!" I yelped, but Jodie held up a hand to silence me.

"What. Did. You tell them. He could *do*?"

I swallowed. "Ride a bike."

Jodie's face remained completely impassive.

After a little while, I began to wonder if she'd even heard me. I was about to say it again, when she finally reacted.

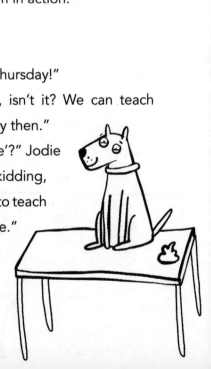

"Ride a bike?" she spluttered. "You told them Destructo could ride a bike!"

"Well, I didn't think they were going to take me seriously, did I?" I protested.

Jodie looked up to the ceiling, then took a deep breath. "What else does the letter say?" she asked.

I glanced down at the page. "Just that they're coming to town to film him in action."

"Oh God. When?"

"Next Thursday."

Jodie flinched. "Next Thursday!"

I nodded. "That's fine, isn't it? We can teach Destructo to ride a bike by then."

"What do you mean 'we'?" Jodie snapped. "And you're kidding, right? It took us two years to teach him not to poo on the table."

"Yes, but he hardly ever does that now," I pointed out. "And riding a bike is easier."

Jodie scowled. "In what world is riding a bike easier than not doing a poo on the table?" She shook her head. "You'll just have to tell them he can't do it."

"But they'll be angry," I protested. "They'll say I wasted their time."

"You did waste their time," Jodie pointed out, heading for the door. "You made this mess, you can clean it up."

"Wait! There's a prize!"

Jodie stopped in the doorway but didn't turn round. "What kind of prize?"

"The most talented pet in each episode gets five thousand quid," I said. "The overall series winner gets twenty thousand and gets patted by the queen. The pet gets patted by the queen, I mean, not the owner. At least, I assume it's the pet."

Jodie didn't say anything at first. She just loomed in the doorway, tapping her foot.

"Twenty-five thousand pounds?" she said eventually.

"If he wins the whole show," I said.

Jodie clicked her tongue. "Nope, still not interested. You're on your own."

"Wait!" I yelped.

Jodie rolled her eyes. "I told you, I'm not doing it."

"No, not that," I said, pointing to my watch. "Leon!"

"Who's Leon?"

Over on my desk, half buried under crisp bags and yet more pants, a ringing sound was coming from my laptop. A photo of the caller appeared in the Skype window. He had curly blond hair, a chiselled jaw, and piercing blue eyes that made Jodie let out a little yelp of surprise.

"Who is that?" she asked.

"That's Leon. That's the guy who emailed me

about Madame Shirley," I said, scrabbling for the laptop.

Jodie got there before I did. Her face bunched up in disgust as she tipped the laptop sideways, chucking the pants on to my bed. She ran a hand through her hair and wiped the flecks of mud off her face while simultaneously clicking the webcam icon.

For a moment there was nothing but a black screen, then Leon was revealed. He was standing in what must have been his bedroom, jogging on the spot. His knees were going very high and just watching him made me instantly exhausted.

"Leon, I presume?" said Jodie.

"That sounded a bit creepy," I told her. She elbowed me in the ribs by way of a reply.

On screen, Leon stopped running and gave us a wave. "Beaky? And you must be Jodie," Leon said in a lilting Scottish accent. "I've read all about you."

"Ahahahaha!" laughed Jodie. It made her sound like a maniac. "I wouldn't pay attention to any of that. So, uh, hi."

"Hi yourself," said Leon. He smiled, and I swear Jodie's eyes practically turned into love hearts.

"Aaaaanyway," I said, angling the laptop towards me. "So ... you can't tell a lie, either?"

"Oh, no, sorry," said Leon, his face falling. "I can lie just fine."

"What?" I said, my heart sinking. "I thought you said you'd been in Madame Shirley's machine?"

"I have," said Leon. "But it didn't make me tell the truth."

Jodie and I looked at each other. "Oh?" Jodie said. "So what did it do to you?"

"Well..." began Leon. And with that, he started to explain.

CHAPTER 3
THE OTHER MACHINE

It turns out that Leon was never a liar. I mean, no worse than anyone else and nowhere near my league. No, Leon's problem was laziness.

He slumped out of bed every morning, rolled into his creased uniform and slouched his way to school after guzzling a Mars Bar for breakfast.

At weekends he'd sleep until one, play his Xbox till three, then spend the rest of the day eating junk food, watching movies and loudly complaining whenever he was asked to empty the dishwasher.

"Didn't your parents mind?" Jodie asked.

"Of course. They hated it! They were always trying to encourage me outside, or dreaming up ways to punish me for leaving a mess everywhere," Leon said. "And that's why, when my mum saw that sign in Madame Shirley's shop window, she dragged me inside."

Jodie and I both leaned closer. "What sign?" asked Jodie.

"'World's Only Anti-Laziness Machine'," Leon whispered. "It was a machine to stop people being lazy," he explained. A bit unnecessarily, I thought.

"What happened?" I asked.

Leon shrugged. "It worked. I came out running. I raced straight home and tidied my room."

"Wow," said Jodie.

"And then I tidied my parents' room, then cleaned all the windows."

I whistled softly through my teeth.

"And then I cut the grass, washed the car and

36

redecorated the kitchen," said Leon. "That was day one."

"When was this?" I asked.

"Two years ago," said Leon.

"Two *years*?" I spluttered. "You've been affected for *two years*?"

"Aye," said Leon, but then he hesitated. "I mean, I *think* so, anyway."

"You've been doing star jumps for the past thirty seconds," I said. "You're definitely still affected."

Leon laughed, looked down and stopped jumping. "What I mean is, I'm not sure if it's the machine any more or if it's just me," he said. "I like the fact I'm not lazy now. I feel great."

"You look *amazing*," said Jodie. She bit her lip. "Wait, did I say that out loud?"

"Yes," I confirmed. "You did."

"I spent the first few weeks trying to track

37

Madame Shirley down, just like you," Leon said. "I hated her for what she'd done to me but after a while ... I dunno. I'm a better person for having been in that machine. She changed my life. I suppose if she walked in here now I'd thank her."

"I'd rugby-tackle her to the ground and tie her up," I said. I blew out my cheeks and shrugged. "Well, this was completely pointless, wasn't it?"

"Beaky!" said Jodie.

"Well, it was!" I insisted. "He doesn't know where Madame Shirley is – you don't, do you?"

"Sorry," said Leon, shaking his head.

"And, as far as he knows, the effect never wears off. So, basically, I'm doomed, and I'll never be able to tell a lie again," I said.

Leon shrugged. "I suppose I just wanted to say ... it gets better, you know? What you're feeling now, I felt that, too. All the time. Twenty-hours a day, since I only sleep for four hours a night now."

"How?" asked Jodie. "You look so … fresh."

"Thanks," said Leon. He flashed her that winning smile again, then turned back to me. "But it gets better, honest. You might not think it now, but maybe someday you'll want to thank her, too."

"I find that very hard to believe," I said.

Leon smiled. "Yeah. I know. But someday."

He gestured with a thumb to his door. "Anyway, I have to go. I've got a sponsored run later and I want to quickly cut the grass and tar the drive first. If you ever want to talk, just call me."

"I definitely will," said Jodie.

"I think he was talking to me," I said.

Jodie blushed. "Oh, yes. I mean he will. Not me. Ahahaha. Yes."

I closed the laptop before she could say anything else. "I did that for your own good," I told her, then I sighed. "What a total waste of time."

"Oh, I don't know," said Jodie. From her face, I

could tell she was already in the process of removing one of the existing Top 5 Boys from her list and replacing his name with Leon's. "It wasn't all bad."

"Help me teach Destructo how to ride a bike, and I'll give you his Skype username," I said.

Jodie thumped me on the leg. It hurt quite a lot.

"Or you can just beat me up and take it," I said. "Whichever you prefer."

I was just wrestling my bike out of the shed when I felt a tap on my shoulder. Mum was standing behind me, smiling in a way that immediately made me think she was up to something.

"Going on a bike ride?" she asked.

"No, it's for Destructo," I said.

"Destructo? He can't ride a bike."

"Well, not *yet*," I said. "I'm going to teach him so he can win *TV's Most Talented Pets*."

"That's nice," she said, not really listening. "Anyway, I need you to do me a small favour."

"What is it?" I asked.

"Nothing major. Just a little thing," said Mum.

"Which is…?"

"Seriously, it's tiny. It's barely even a favour at all," she insisted.

"Just tell me," I said, getting suspicious.

"I need you to come campaigning with me," said Mum. "Door to door."

"Ugh," I groaned. "Not this again."

Mum had been a member of the school's Parent Teacher Association for the past three years, and had put herself forward to be the new chairperson after the last one had either dropped out or dropped dead. I could never remember which.

The trouble was, Mrs Green, one of the other

parents – and Evie's mum – had also put herself forward for the position, and now she and Mum were locked in a ridiculous battle for the job.

Jodie and I kept finding ourselves caught in the middle of it. If she wasn't getting us to help her print out leaflets, Mum was testing her speeches on us, forcing us to brainstorm "issues" and generally making us work as an unpaid political campaign team.

Going door-to-door campaigning, though? That was too far.

"No," I said. "No way."

"Why not?" Mum asked.

"Because I don't want to," I said bluntly. "Also, because it's insane – you're trying to be the head of the PTA, not the Prime Minister.

And because I'll end up looking like an idiot."

"No, you won't!" Mum insisted. "You just helped the school win the Winston and ... whatever-it's-called Cup for the first time *ever*. They won't think you're an idiot, they'll think you're a hero!"

"I still don't want to," I said. "I want to teach Destructo how to ride a bike."

Mum, sensibly, chose to completely ignore this.

"I'll give all your chores to Jodie for a whole day," she said. "No emptying the dishwasher, no picking up the dog poo from the garden … or off the table."

"He hardly ever does that any more," I pointed out. "And no, I still don't want to do it."

"OK, I'll give Jodie all your chores for a *week*."

I almost caved then. A week without having to lift a finger around the house was sorely tempting but I could tell Mum was desperate.

"A month," I said.

"Ha! No way!" Mum said, then she tutted below her breath. "A fortnight. Final offer."

"Deal!" I said.

Mum nodded. "Good." She dumped one of my old school bags into my arms and I almost collapsed under the weight of it. "You can carry the leaflets."

CHAPTER 4
THE ENEMY

One hour later I was regretting letting Mum talk me into it. She'd made a list of the parents she considered to be the most influential in the school, and so far we'd visited about a dozen different houses, where she'd paraded me like a trophy and made me tell the story about winning the WAWWCOCC for the school.

She had tried to get me to tell the parents how proud I was of both her and the PTA in general, but after the third time of me changing "proud" to "deeply ashamed", she knocked that idea on the head and just made me focus on the cup-winning stuff.

"This is going quite well, isn't it?" she trilled, leading me away from the twelfth bewildered parent of the evening.

"Not really," I said. "I'm cold and hungry, and everyone we've spoken to thinks you're a lunatic."

"Hahahahahahaha!" Mum laughed, the sound going on for far too long and becoming increasingly high-pitched. "No, they don't! They think I'm invested in the success of the PTA. They think I'm enthusiastic!"

"Enthusiastically insane, maybe," I said. "Can we please go home now?"

"Not quite," said Mum. "There's just one last house left to go to. Mr Lawson's."

"Mr Lawson's?" I gasped. "As in, the head teacher Mr Lawson? Why are we going there? He can't vote for the PTA head, can he?"

"No, but he's very influential in the school," said Mum. "If I get him on side, he could help me beat that awful Green woman."

"Why do you keep calling her that?" I sighed. "You used to be friends."

"Yes. *Used to be*," said Mum, her lips going all puckered and thin. "Before she decided to trample all over our friendship by standing against me for the PTA position."

"Seems like a silly thing to throw away a friendship for," I said. "You know, considering no one even cares about the PTA."

"Oh, Dylan," she said, putting a hand on my shoulder and smiling at me in that way grown-ups do when they're about to say something really patronizing. "You'll understand when you're older."

She ruffled my hair, then crisply about-turned and hurried along the street. "Now come on, Mr Lawson's house is just…"

Mum stopped as she rounded a bend in the road. Her eyes went very wide, then very narrow.

There, standing at the other end of the street, staring back, was Mrs Green. Evie stood beside her, a shopping bag slung over her shoulder. Even from this distance, I could tell it was filled with campaign leaflets.

"I don't believe it!" said Mum. Along the street, Mrs Green's lips moved in perfect time with Mum's words. "What's she doing here?"

"Same as you, probably," I said.

At that, Mum's eyes darted to a house halfway along the road.

"Come on, Dylan!" she hissed, breaking into a run, and looking completely ridiculous as she *clopped* along in her high heels.

Mrs Green broke into some undignified lumbering of her own, as both she and Mum raced towards Mr Lawson's house.

"Well this is humiliating," I muttered, swinging the bag on to my back and trudging after Mum.

By the time I caught up with her, she was right outside Mr Lawson's garden, standing nose to nose with Mrs Green. They both had a hand on the front gate, and were taking it in turns to push and pull it, so the gate hadn't moved an inch.

"What are you doing, Claire?" hissed Mrs Green. "Let go."

"You let go, Helen. I'm just here to say hello to Mr Lawson," growled Mum.

"Oh, really? Well, that's a coincidence, because so am I!"

"I was here first!"

"No, *I* was!"

Evie walked over and stood beside me as our mums continued to argue. "All right?" she said.

"Been better, to be honest," I admitted. "Think they'll start fighting?"

"I hope not," said Evie. "Didn't you say your mum was a tae kwon do champion?"

I smiled. "Probably. She isn't, though. She thinks tae kwon do is the name of a Korean gymnast."

Evie laughed. "Funny."

"It's true!" I said.

"My mum thinks 'kung fu' is a type of Chinese food," Evie said. "Whenever we get a takeaway she asks for the kung-fu chicken."

"Wow."

"I know, right?" Evie grinned. "She refused to let me watch *Kung Fu Panda* because she thought the panda got eaten at the end."

I laughed so loudly that both Mum and Mrs Green's heads snapped in our direction. For a moment they stared at us disapprovingly, then they got stuck straight back into arguing.

"I don't even know why you put yourself forward," Mum spat. "You missed half the meetings last year."

"How would you know? You were never there!" yelled Mrs Green.

"How dare you? I've *literally* given my blood, sweat and tears for the PTA!" snapped Mum.

I leaned closer to Evie and whispered, "As well as not knowing what tae kwon do is, my mum also doesn't understand the meaning of the word 'literally'."

"Oh yes?" shrieked Mrs Green. "Well, I've *literally* given my whole life to it!"

"Nor does mine," said Evie.

The front door to Mr Lawson's house opened. In a flash, Mum and Mrs Green transformed their scowls into warm smiles, expecting to see Mr Lawson standing there.

Instead, it was Wayne. "D'you mind keeping the noise down?" he said, scowling.

"Ah, Wayne!" said Mum.

"Lovely Wayne!" added Mrs Green.

"Is your dad in?" they both asked at once.

Wayne shook his head. "Nah. He's visiting my brother."

"In prison," I added helpfully.

"Oh," said Mrs Green.

"Right," said Mum.

They both pushed for the gate and spoke at the same time. "Well, maybe I could just leave this leaflet?"

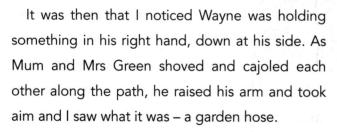

It was then that I noticed Wayne was holding something in his right hand, down at his side. As Mum and Mrs Green shoved and cajoled each other along the path, he raised his arm and took aim and I saw what it was – a garden hose.

A spray of water shot from the nozzle, blasting both mums in the face and upper body. They screamed and wailed, flailing their arms in front of themselves as they stumbled backwards, shouting, "Stop!" and "Cut it out!" and "My new shoes!" in increasingly desperate tones.

Wayne released the trigger and the water stopped.

"Whoops, sorry," he said. He lowered his arm and pointed the nozzle at a potted plant on the doorstep. "I was trying to water this. It accidentally went off in my hand."

He gave the plant the briefest of squirts, nodded once in my and Evie's direction, then closed the door. Mum and Mrs Green hurried out of the garden, frantically drying their faces on their sleeves and smearing make-up everywhere in the process. Evie and I stared at them for a few seconds, open-mouthed with shock, then erupted in fits of laughter.

"Why are you laughing? It's not funny!" cried Mum.

"It's *hilarious*!" I said.

"We're completely drenched!" Mrs Green yelped.

"Yeah. That's pretty much nailed why we're laughing," Evie giggled.

"Come on, you must see the funny side!" I said.

From the expression on their faces, though, it quickly became clear that they didn't see the funny side. At all.

Our laughter fizzled out and I quietly cleared my throat. "Or, y'know, maybe you don't," I said.

Mrs Green glared at me.

Mum glared at Evie.

"Come on, Dylan. We're leaving," Mum said.

"Yes, come away, Evie," said Mrs Green, beckoning Evie to her side. "I can see we're going to have to be more careful about the company you keep."

"I was just thinking the same thing," said Mum. "Here, Dylan. Now."

Evie shot me a glance. "Uh, I guess I'll see you at—"

"No time for chit-chat, Evie," said Mrs Green.

Evie rolled her eyes, then gave me a wave. I waved back, then yelped as Mum caught me by the arm and started marching me off along the street. "I think it'd be best if you don't hang around with that girl any more," said Mum.

"*That girl* is my friend!" I protested.

Mum shook her head. "It's like that old saying –
'The daughter of my enemy is my enemy.'"

"But Mrs Green isn't my enemy! She's *your*
enemy, for some reason."

"Well, it's like that other old saying, then – 'The
daughter of my mother's enemy is my enemy.'"

"That's not a saying," I said.

"It is now," said Mum, releasing my arm and
squelching off ahead of me. "In fact, I might even
get it put on a poster."

"Yep," I whispered, shoving my hands into my
pockets and following her. "She's finally lost her
mind."

CHAPTER 5
REHEARSAL #1

Next morning I stood in the garden, yawning and trying to remember how my eyes worked. Destructo sat on the grass in front of me, his head cocked quizzically to one side. Beside him was my bike, propped up against the side of the bin.

"Come on, it's riding a bike," I muttered, wiping the crusts of sleep from my eyes. "It's not rocket science!"

By the time we'd got home last night and had all listened to

Mum ranting about Mrs Green, Evie, Wayne and anything else that came to mind, it was too late to start Destructo's training. Instead I set my alarm for 5 a.m., thinking I could spend half an hour or so showing Destructo the basics of riding a bike, then leave him practising while I went in and had breakfast.

In the cold light of day – although technically it was still pretty dark – I could see it wouldn't be quite so simple. The only interest Destructo had shown in the bike so far was right after I'd propped it up, when he'd peed on the pedals.

I pointed to the saddle. "On," I instructed, in what I hoped was a commanding tone. "On the bike. Get on. Get on the bike. Bike. On. Get. The. Oh, *come on*!"

For the third time since I'd come outside, I took hold of the handlebars and ordered Destructo to watch closely. He wagged his tail as I very deliberately swung my leg over the bar and slid back on to the saddle.

"See? Easy. I've been able to do this since I was six!"

I hopped off and pointed to the saddle again. "Your turn."

Destructo didn't move.

"Right, fine," I sighed, reaching into my pocket. "Will you do it for a biscuit?"

I brought out the bone-shaped dog-treat. Destructo immediately snatched it from my fingers and swallowed it whole. He sat down again, eyeing my pocket expectantly and licking his chops.

"Going well?"

I turned to find Jodie standing on the back step, a mug in her hand.

"Not really," I admitted.

"Yeah, didn't think so," she said. "By the way, you know Mum said I'd do all your chores for a fortnight?"

I grinned. "Oh yes!"

"Yeah, not happening," said Jodie.

"But…"

Jodie gave me the evil eye.

"OK, fair enough," I muttered, then I turned back to Destructo, who was busy licking his foot. "I don't understand it. Why won't he get on the bike?" I asked.

"Um, because he's a dog?" Jodie suggested. "They're actually pretty renowned for *not* getting on bikes."

"I even tried to bribe him with one of these," I said, taking another biscuit from my pocket. Destructo immediately jumped up and gobbled it. "That does it," I said. "I'm lifting him on."

"Good luck with that," said Jodie.

I tried to wrap my arms round Destructo but my hands didn't quite meet in the middle. "Right, I'll just…" I grunted, trying to get a proper hold on him. "Maybe this way will…"

An enormous pink tongue slobbered inside my ear. "Aah! Cut it out!" I said, turning to try to heave him over my shoulder. I felt a sudden rustling in my pocket and looked down to find Destructo wolfing down the rest of the biscuits.

"Hey, get off!" I said, putting him down. Destructo crunched happily on his stolen treats.

"Well?" asked Jodie. "How did that go, do you think?"

"It could've gone better," I admitted.

"Still, at least he didn't try to eat the bike."

There was a *bang* as Destructo sunk his teeth into the front wheel.

I sighed. "He's trying to eat the bike."

"Destructo, no!" said Jodie.

Destructo immediately stopped chewing on the tyre and lay down, looking guilty.

"He listens to you. You have to help me," I said.

"Not happening," said Jodie. She took another sip and peered at me over the rim of her mug. "By the way, how are you feeling about Mum banning you from talking to Evie?" she asked.

"Hmm?" I mumbled, playing for time as my fingers quietly snuck into my pocket – the one that wasn't currently filled with crumbs and dog slobber.

"You like her, don't you?" Jodie said.

"Who, Mum?"

"Evie!"

"Oh. As I told Theo, yes, she has many fine qualities," I said.

"No, I mean you *really* like her."

At that, I whipped out my gobstopper and crammed it in my mouth.

Jodie grinned and started to sing. "Beaky's got a girlfriend, Beaky's got a girlfriend."

"Nngg, ayf dmnt!"

"Yeah, whatever," Jodie said. She shrugged, then went back inside, leaving me with Destructo.

"Famps fr yu elp," I said, then I spat the gobstopper into its bag and shoved it back in my pocket.

I gazed down at Destructo. He looked back up at me, his tongue hanging out.

"This could be even harder than I thought," I said. I tossed him the last of the biscuit crumbs and headed inside for breakfast.

CHAPTER 6
REHEARSAL #2

The rest of the day passed in a blur of bleary eyes and yawning. Unsurprisingly it turns out that I don't cope well with getting up at 5 a.m., and I fell asleep in English (once), geography (twice) and modern studies (the whole period).

Luckily Theo woke me up each time by kicking me hard on the shin under the desk. I don't know what I'd do without him. Apart from have fewer bruises, I mean.

In the afternoon, we were let out of lessons for the second play rehearsal. Everyone was already up on stage by the time Theo and I made it to the hall. Evie grinned when she saw us. I smiled back, even though I was half-expecting Mum to come running out from behind the stage curtains to tell me off.

Ms Brannan shrieked theatrically and did a little dance to celebrate our arrival. "Aha! And with that, our company is once more complete," she said, sweeping her arm in front of her and bowing low. "M'lords."

"Er ... all right?" I said, sidestepping past her and running up the stairs at the side of the stage.

"Before we start our rehearsal," said Ms Brannan, "there are a couple of things I want to talk about. One – ticket sales. They went on sale yesterday and they are being snapped up! They are *flying*."

I let out a groan. "Seriously? You mean people

are actually going to come and see me doing this?"

It wasn't that I didn't like performing, it was just that the rumours about me and Evie had started doing the rounds through the whole school (I blamed Theo) and being the romantic lead opposite her was... Well, it was going to be embarrassing. The fewer people who saw the play, the better.

"Oh yes, indeedy!" said Ms Brannan. "We've sold almost three so far!"

Chloe, who was standing at the back of the stage and scrolling through her phone, looked up. "*Almost* three?" Her lips moved silently, like she was counting in her head. "So ... two?"

"Yes! Which isn't half bad!"

"It's not great, either, is it?" I asked. "Although the fewer the merrier, as far as I'm concerned."

"We've still got a few days until curtain up.

There's plenty of time for sales to pick up," the teacher insisted. "Anyway, thing *numero* two. We need to pick out costumes. Dylan, Evie, why don't you go below stage and see what you can find."

I blinked in surprise. "Sorry?"

"You and Evie. Pop below the stage and bring up the costume box."

I looked at Evie, then stared at the stage floor, as if I could see through it with X-ray vision.

"Together?" I said.

"Yes."

"Me and Evie?" I said.

"Yes! Is there a problem?"

I looked to Theo for help but he just grinned back at me and rocked on his heels.

Evie jumped down off the stage and landed with an echoing *thunk* on the hall's wooden floor. She drummed her hands on the front of the stage and looked up at me.

66

"You coming?"

I slowly descended the steps until I was standing next to her.

"Um…"

"Wait!" said Chloe, looking up from her phone again. "What's happening?"

"They're going to get costumes," said Duncan. It was rare that he worked up the courage to speak but I realized Wayne was nowhere to be seen, so that explained it.

Chloe barged to the front of the stage.

"Over my dead body. They're not choosing the costumes – *I am*," she said.

"It's fine, Chloe, we—" Evie began, before being abruptly cut off.

"Uh, *hello*? Costume designer," Chloe said, pointing to herself.

"Wardrobe assistant," Ms Brannan corrected.

"Same thing," said Chloe, waving a hand dismissively in the teacher's direction. "And as the costume designer, I'm not having you two picking your own outfits. Beaky, you go down and bring up all the costumes you can find. I'll handle everything from there."

Evie shrugged. "Fine," she said, opening the little door at the front of the stage.

"Not you," said Chloe. "You need to stay here so we can think about what we're doing with your make-up."

"I don't think we need worry too much about that yet," said Ms Brannan.

"Seriously, Miss?" Chloe said. "Have you seen her face? No offence, Evie. We need to establish a colour scheme, run greasepaint tests, decide if we're shaving her head…"

"We're definitely not," said Evie.

"We'll talk about that later," said Chloe. "As the make-up artist—"

"Wardrobe assistant."

"Whatever. As the make-up artist, it's my job to

worry about this stuff." She studied Evie's face and sucked air in through her teeth. "And I am *worried*. Still, at least you're playing an alien. You should suit that. No offence, Evie."

"None taken," said Evie. "Well, maybe a bit."

"No, I don't mean it like *that*," said Chloe. "I mean, you're beautiful. In your own way. Gorgeous. In your own way. Isn't she, Beaky?"

Everyone turned to look at me except Evie, who blushed a little and took a sudden interest in the ceiling.

My mouth flapped open and closed. "I … uh … I … uh …"

There was no time to grab for my gobstopper. Ducking low, I hurled myself through the door in the front of the stage, fell down some steps and landed on a large mattress. Unfortunately it was a prop mattress made of wood, so it hurt quite a lot.

"Are you OK, Dylan?" asked Ms Brannan, thrusting her head through the doorway. From my position, flat on my back, I managed a shaky thumbs up. "What on Earth did you do that for?"

I answered honestly – as ever – but in a way that avoided embarrassing myself further. "It seemed like a good idea at the time, Miss."

"Do you want some help?"

"No!" I spluttered. I scrambled to my feet. "No, I'm fine."

"Right you are," Ms Brannan said. "I'll leave you to it."

She backed out of the doorway and I turned to survey the under-stage area. The ceiling wasn't quite so low that I had to duck, but low enough that I found myself ducking anyway, just in case.

The whole place was a clutter of boxes, bits of old set, disused props, lighting rigs, and what could generously be described as "stuff", but more accurately described as "junk". The only light in the place came from the doorway I'd just dived through, and everything more than a metre away was shrouded in shadow.

"Right, costumes. Costumes. Where would they keep the costumes?" I wondered.

There was a large cardboard box near the back wall that looked as good a place to start as any. I picked my way across to it, clambering over old stage curtains, a couple of dusty speakers and a paper-mâché chicken wearing a bowler hat.

The further I got from the door, the darker it became. I was busy trying not to think about spiders leaping out of the shadows when I heard a rush of footsteps right behind me.

"Wah!" I yelped, spinning on the spot. "H-hello?" I whispered into the gloom.

Then the footsteps came again, louder this time. A flurry of dust fell from the ceiling, and I realized the sound I'd heard was someone walking across the stage.

Sighing with relief, I turned back to the box, only for a monstrously ugly figure to explode from inside, waving its arms above its head and roaring like a wild animal.

My scream was so high-pitched I'm surprised the glass in the lighting rigs didn't shatter. I stumbled back, tripped on the model chicken, and flattened it as I fell.

"Oh man, your face!" said Wayne, pulling off a monster mask to reveal his gleeful grin. "You should have seen your face!"

"You nearly gave me a heart attack!" I gasped.

"Sorry," Wayne said. "No, wait... I'm not. That was brilliant."

"What are you doing down here?" I asked, struggling to my feet.

"Waiting to jump out on whoever Brannan sent

down for the costumes," Wayne said.

"How long have you been here?"

"Not long," said Wayne, tossing the mask over his shoulder. "Just since second period."

"Second period? That's before break!" I spluttered. "You've been hiding in that box for nearly three hours! That's insane."

"It was totally worth it," said Wayne. "Your face!"

He chuckled for a few more seconds, then jabbed a thumb in the direction of an ancient wardrobe. "It's in there," he said.

"What is?" I asked. "Narnia?"

"The costume stuff," Wayne said. He pulled open the door and there, hanging in front of us, was a costume.

A dog costume.

A big grey dog costume.

Although I didn't fully realize it at the time, somewhere, at the back of my mind, an idea began to form.

73

CHAPTER 7

BETRAYED

The first half of the rehearsal was spent strutting up and down the stage in a variety of weird outfits, while Chloe criticized everything about us.

The way Evie walked was a problem. One of my arms looked longer than the other. The girl who was playing my mum had – and I quote – "a face like a human foot".

Chloe didn't stop there, either. Duncan had fat knees. A girl called Jenna apparently looked like she was choking on a hamster, although I couldn't see it myself.

Even when she was being complimentary, Chloe still somehow managed to sound mean. She told one guy that he had the "perfect body" for his role. Unfortunately his role was an alien slime monster with a giant zit for a head. He left the hall in tears.

With the costumes finally chosen, Chloe set to work to make them look more space-age. This basically seemed to involve gluing little silver moons and stars to them, from what I could gather. While she was busy doing that (with Wayne helping) we were finally able to squeeze in some rehearsing.

As soon as we finished, I raced home to fit in an hour of bike training with Destructo. I tried to convince Theo to help me but he had a dentist appointment. Or so he said.

The bike practice went pretty much exactly the same way the morning session had done, except this time Destructo chewed the back tyre rather than the front, and it took me longer to prise it from his massive jaws.

During dinner, Dad unveiled his new theme song for *TV's Most Talented Pets*. He didn't have his xylophone so he tapped the beat on the salt cellar with his knife and fork instead.

"Pets. Pets, pets, pets,
P-p-p-pets. Pets, pets,
Pets,
Including cats,
Pets, pets, d-pets,
P-p-pets,
Pets!"

He gave a little bow at the end. "Well?"

"So, instead of singing the word 'dogs' over and over again, you sing 'pets' over and over again?" said Jodie.

"The 'including cats' bit doesn't really fit the

rhythm very well," I pointed out.

"Yes, it does," he said.

Jodie and I both shook our heads.

"They're right, it doesn't," Mum agreed.

Dad sniffed. "Well, I'm the only professional musician in the family, so I think I know best." He spent the next few minutes pushing a chunk of courgette around his plate in silence ... which left a gap for Mum to jump in.

"So?" she said, raising her eyebrows at me. "How was school?"

"Fine," I said.

Jodie shrugged. "All right."

"Speak to anyone?" Mum asked.

"Lots of people," I said.

"Uh-huh," said Mum. "Good. Good." She picked up a baby carrot and bit the end off it. "Anyone in particular?"

I sighed and set my cutlery down on the table. "Do you mean, was I speaking to Evie?"

"Were you?" asked Mum, her eyes narrowing.

"Yes!" I said. "We held hands and I told her I loved her!"

Mum's jaw flopped open. Dad stopped pushing his dinner around. Even Jodie looked up from her plate in surprise.

"And then a spaceship crashed and Tomulax, the High Emperor of Artribius IV, tried to shoot us both with a ray gun."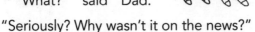

"What?" said Dad. "Seriously? Why wasn't it on the news?"

"Because it was in the play! We're doing the school play together," I said. "*Romeo and Juliet.*"

"Oh," said Dad. He frowned. "Are there ray guns in *Romeo and Juliet*?"

"There are since Ms Brannan got her hands on it," I said. "But yes, Mum, in answer to your question, I did speak to Evie today."

"I see. I see," said Mum. "Do you know another

of Shakespeare's plays?" she said. "It's... Well, I forget the name, but it's about Julius Caesar. You know what happens in it?"

"Something boring no one understands?" I guessed.

"He gets stabbed in the back. Right in the back," said Mum. "Betrayed by those closest to him. Ring any bells, Dylan? Know anyone else who has betrayed the trust of those closest to them recently? Hmm? Someone sitting at this table, maybe? Someone sitting *in your seat right now*?"

"Is it me?" I asked.

"Yes, it's you!" said Mum. "I ask you to do one thing – one little thing..."

"Stop talking to my friend because you and her mum have fallen out over the stupid PTA," I said.

"Exactly! One little... And it's not stupid, Dylan. One little thing and you won't do it."

"That's not really fair, Mum," said Jodie, coming

to my defence. "They're in the play together. And she's kind of his girlfriend."

"What!" Mum spluttered, almost choking on a piece of potato.

"She is not!" I protested.

"She totally is," Jodie sniggered. "Beaky's got a girlfriend, Beaky's got a girlfriend…"

"At least I didn't get caught kissing Bradley Wells in the science corridor at break time!" I blurted, then immediately clamped my hand over my mouth.

It was true. Jodie *had* been caught kissing a boy from her year in the science corridor at break time the day before. She must have thought I didn't know or she wouldn't have dared to start teasing me about Evie.

"And he's not even in her creepy Top Five Boys list," I added, although it was a bit muffled by my hand.

Mum and Dad both turned to Jodie. "Is that true, Jodie?" Mum asked.

"No!" said Jodie.

"Yes!" I insisted. "Bradley's mate Cyril saw them, and he told Theo's cousin Suzanne, who told Theo's other cousin Julian, who told Theo, who told me."

"Any or all of those people could have been lying," babbled Jodie. "And they definitely were. Probably Cyril. I've never trusted him. He's shifty, if you ask me." She got up from the table. "Anyway, I've got a lot of homework. Thanks for a lovely meal!"

We all watched her dart out of the room. Three seconds later, her bedroom door slammed shut.

"Who's Bradley Wells?" asked Dad.

I reached across and patted his hand. "Trust me. You don't want to know."

"Fine," said Mum.

I raised an eyebrow. "Fine?"

81

"You can talk to Evie Green. I didn't realize she was your girlfriend."

"She isn't!"

Mum smiled in a really patronizing sort of way. "Well, whatever. Just promise you won't reveal any of my campaign strategies."

"OK, first of all, I don't know or care what any of your campaign strategies are," I said. "And secondly, I was going to talk to her anyway, even though she's not – I repeat, *not* – my girlfriend." I stood up and flashed Mum a grin. "But thanks all the same."

And then, before anyone suggested it should be my turn to do the dishes, I left the room, took the stairs two at a time and darted into my bedroom, only for something to *thwack* me across the head from behind.

OW!

CHAPTER 8

EXPERIMENTING

I ducked, covering my head with my hands, then turned to find Jodie standing behind me, clutching one of my trainers.

"Ow! Did you just hit me with a shoe?"

"Yes," she seethed, closing the door to block my exit. "You're lucky I couldn't find your baseball bat."

"It's under the bed," I said before I could stop myself.

Jodie glanced down at the space beneath the

bed but luckily there was a force field of dirty pants on the floor right in front of it.

"For your information, I did *not* kiss Bradley Wells in the science corridor," she told me. "It was Dawn."

"You kissed *Dawn* in the science corridor?"

"No! Dawn kissed Bradley Wells in the science corridor!"

"Oh. Right," I said. "So who did you kiss, then?"

"No one!"

I sat down at my desk. "But if it's not true, how could I say it?" I asked.

Jodie shrugged. "How should I know? Did you think it was true?"

"Yeah," I said, nodding.

"Well, that must be it, then. You thought it was true, so you could say it. Try now. Now that you know it definitely is *not* true and that I wouldn't kiss Bradley Wells if you paid me and gave me fake lips."

"You k-k-k…" I stammered. "You *k-k-k*… You're right, I can't say it. But wait, let's try an experiment."

"Does it involve cutting you open like a frog?" Jodie asked. "If so, I'm in."

"No, not that sort of experiment."

I tore a page from a notebook, then hurriedly wrote a few lines. Jumping up, I stood next to Jodie and angled the paper so she could see it. Her name was on the top with a line of text below it. Beneath that was my name, then another line.

"What's this?" Jodie asked.

"It's a script. Read your line."

"What? I'm not reading…" She tutted and rolled her eyes. "Fine. *I did not kiss Bradley Wells in the science corridor.*"

I took a deep breath. This was it – the next words out of my mouth might well determine the entire course of my life from that moment on.

"Yes, Jodie, you did."

The paper slipped from my fingers and fluttered to the floor. I turned to Jodie, my eyes wide. "I told a lie! Jodie, I told a lie!"

Jodie looked down at the paper in surprise. "What? But … I mean… How?"

"Because I can read a script!"

"But that's not a script. That's real stuff," Jodie pointed out.

"I *know*, but I turned it into a script and then I could say it! This is *amazing*!"

I spent a few seconds dancing round the room, then stopped. "Wait," I said. "Let's test something."

I picked up the paper and memorized my line, word for word. "OK, say it again."

Jodie sighed. "I did not kiss Bradley Wells in the science corridor."

"No, Jodie, you did not!" I agreed.

I punched the air in triumph.

A moment later, I froze. "Wait, that's not right. I was supposed to say you did."

"Looks like you can only lie if you're reading the script," Jodie said.

I flopped down on to my chair again. "I really hoped that was going to work."

"It's better than nothing," Jodie said. "Maybe you can still use it."

"Yeah. Maybe."

I turned away to hide my misery and tapped the touchpad of my laptop. It was an old one of Dad's, and complained noisily about being woken up.

"Well, I'll leave you to it," said Jodie.

"Yeah, you probably should," I said glumly. "I'm about to do a massive fart."

Jodie left.

I did a massive fart.

The laptop's screen flickered into life and the speakers gave a tinny-sounding *ping* as an email arrived in my inbox. It was from *TV's Most Talented Pets*.

I clicked the subject line, hoping the email was going to tell me the whole thing had been called off. But nope. It was a follow-up confirmation of the date, time and location for the filming – 5 p.m. next Thursday in our manky local church hall (it didn't actually say "manky" in the email) – and some details about the people and pets taking part.

My name was there, of course, along with the name of my school. A little blurb below my name read:

Pet name – Destructo

Pet type – Dog

Pet talent – Bike Riding

The next name was Sebastian Farrinton, who I'd never heard of. He was from Foxley Hill, the school we'd beaten in the Winston and Watson cup. His pet details were:

Pet name – Gavin

Pet type – Wasp

Pet talent – Tying knots

"*Wasp?*" I said out loud.

"What kind of weirdo has a pet wasp?"

It was the last name on the list that really took me by surprise, though.

Evie Green.

"Seriously?" I said, out loud. First the PTA thing, then the play, and now this. It was as if the whole world was trying to force us together.

Apparently Evie had a cat called Gizmo who could play the drums. Between that, the knot-tying wasp and Destructo's promised bike antics, the producers must have been feeling pretty good about their upcoming episode.

Little did they know, of course, that Destructo couldn't even get on a bike, let alone ride one. But that was about to change. I closed my laptop and jumped to my feet.

That dog was going to learn to ride a bike.

Tonight.

Even if it killed me.

CHAPTER 9
DEVIOUS SCHEMES

Destructo didn't learn to ride a bike that night. Fortunately it didn't kill me, although at times I almost wished it would.

After he'd chewed through another tyre, I'd come to the conclusion that it wasn't going to happen. That meant I could either admit to the show's producer that I'd made the whole thing up or try to come up with a Plan B. Luckily I already had the beginnings of a Plan B at the back of my mind. But I was going to need some help.

Wayne sat across the table from me in the school dinner hall, a Roast Beef flavour Monster Munch halfway to his mouth. We'd  been given the day off lessons for a play rehearsal and had spent most of the morning running through it over and over again, scripts in hand.

After lunch we were supposed to be doing it without the script, which was going to be a problem.

Right now, though, the TV show was the biggest of my many worries.

"You want me to *what*?" said Wayne.

"Dress up as a dog and ride a bike," I said.

Wayne looked to my left, where Theo was sitting. Theo nodded and smiled, which only made Wayne's scowl deepen.

"Why?"

"For the TV."

"Wait… Are you on this talented pet show thing, too? With Evie?" said Wayne.

I quickly reached for my gobstopper in case

91

Wayne asked me about my feelings for Evie but fortunately he was still too puzzled by the whole dog/bike situation to ask me about her.

"Yeah," I said. "I told them my dog could ride a bike."

"And can it?"

"Of course he can't!" I said. "That's why I need you to dress up."

"Why can't he do it?" Wayne asked, nodding at Theo.

"He's already got a job to do," I said.

"What about your sister? Ask her."

"I asked her on the way to school this morning," I said. "But she punched me in the stomach and pushed me into a hedge."

Wayne nodded appreciatively. "I like her style." He shoved the Monster Munch in his mouth and leaned back in his chair. "What's in it for me?"

"You get to be on telly."

"Dressed as a dog, so no one knows it's me," Wayne said. "Nice try. Next."

"Think of it as repaying a favour," I said. "Remember when I climbed that tree so you wouldn't humiliate yourself in front of Chloe?"

"I do remember that," said Wayne. "And I repay you every day by not punching your face in."

"He has a point," said Theo.

"Fine." I sighed. "What do you want?"

Wayne leaned forwards and clasped his hands on the table in front of him. "Half the prize money."

"What? No way!" I spluttered.

"Fine. Suit yourself. Good luck finding someone else," said Wayne, getting up.

"Wait!" I said. Wayne hesitated, then sat down. "If I win, you can have a hundred quid."

"A hundred? Out of five grand? No chance. A thousand."

"Two hundred."

"One thousand two hundred."

"What? That's not how negotiation works," I protested.

"One thousand three hundred."

"No, listen…"

"One thousand *four* hundred."

"All right, fine, fine, stop! A thousand pounds. *If* I win. And you can't tell anyone."

Wayne grinned, showing teeth caked in Monster Munch. "Deal," he said.

"OK, good." I glanced around the hall to make sure no one was watching, then took a large piece of paper from my pocket and unfolded it. It was covered in notes, scribbles and diagrams, and represented two full hours of scheming. "Here's what we're going to do…"

With the telly-show situation taken care of, it was time to deal with the problem of having to read the script to say my lines. Fortunately Theo had helped me come up with a plan.

Ms Brannan peered down her nose at me and tapped her foot. "What do you mean, you can't say your lines?"

"I mean I can't say my lines, Miss," I said, hoping that would clear things up. It didn't.

"Why ever not? The play's in two days!"

I shoved my gobstopper in my mouth and let Theo take over. "He's had a head injury, Miss."

Ms Brannan's eyes widened. "A head injury? When?"

"When he was a baby," said Theo. "He got kicked by a horse."

"He got kicked by a *horse*?" the teacher gasped. "In the head? As a *baby*? Oh, Dylan, you poor thing."

"Ah dnt rlly," I mumbled through the gobstopper. "H's tkng rbish."

"He doesn't like to talk about it," Theo said quickly. "That's why he didn't tell you he couldn't memorize his lines. He was too embarrassed."

"Oh, you dotty dumpling!" said Ms Brannan. "Being kicked in the head by a horse as a baby is nothing to be ashamed of. It wasn't your fault!" She glanced at Theo. "It wasn't, was it?"

"No, Miss," Theo said. "Anyway, we've come up with a plan. I'll stand in the wings and hold up his lines on a big card. He can just read them – but, you know, doing an actor voice and everything – and no one will be any the wiser."

"But you're supposed to be on lighting," said Ms Brannan.

"I can just switch them on at the start, then stick them off at the end. Easy," Theo said. "To be honest, I was planning on sleeping through most of it, anyway."

Ms Brannan stroked her chin and looked at me. "Do you think it'll work?"

I nodded enthusiastically. "Es iss."

"Very well. But I do wish you'd told me sooner," she said.

"Yeah, he's sorry about that," said Theo. "Oh, and one other thing. Because it brings back bad memories, we probably shouldn't speak about the horse thing again. Ever."

Ms Brannan looked confused, but then shrugged. "Fine. I won't mention it." She about-turned and clapped her hands. "OK, places, everyone, places. We're going to take this from the top!"

I spat my gobstopper back into my bag and gave Theo a high-five.

Evie met me at the top of the stage steps. "Excited about being on the telly?" she asked.

"Yes!" I said, grinning. I *was* excited, although it was more a nervous excitement than an *excited* excitement. Borderline terror, really. Wayne wasn't exactly the most reliable person in the world and my entire plan hinged on him.

Still, five thousand pounds. Maybe even twenty-five thousand. It was worth the risk.

"You?" I asked.

"Yeah. I've been practising with Gizmo every night. She can do a full four-minute drum solo now," said Evie. "Mind you, not as impressive as your dog riding a bike. I can't wait to see that."

"He can't," I said, before I could stop myself.

"Can't what?"

"Ride a bike. My dog can't ride a bike," I revealed, lowering my voice to a whisper. "I made it up. I've convinced Wayne to dress up as him using one of the costumes from the play."

"You've convinced Wayne to dress up as *your dog* and go on TV?"

I bit my lip. "Yep."

Evie glanced up at the back of the hall where Wayne was busy painting a big cardboard UFO. She exploded into laughter. "Oh man, Beaky, that's the best thing I've ever heard. You're amazing!"

She stuttered to a stop and blushed. "Your plan, I mean. Your plan's amazing. Now I *really* can't wait for tomorrow."

"Come on, chop-chop, places, places!" urged Ms Brannan.

Evie began to turn away, then stopped. "Maybe, you know, if you're not busy, maybe after the filming we could maybe go and maybe hang out for a bit, maybe? If you're not too busy."

"Uh, yeah," I said, but it came out all squeaky, so I tried again. "Uh, yeah. Yeah, that would be … nice."

Evie smiled. "Well… OK, then. Good. You can tell me how you convinced Wayne to dress up as your dog."

"OK!" I said.

"Right, then!" said Evie.

She nodded at me, clicked her fingers a few times, then darted into the wings to get ready. I watched her go, then almost jumped out of my skin when Theo's voice whispered in my ear.

"Beaky and Evie, sitting in a tree…"

Evie's head appeared suddenly through the side curtains. Theo leaped back like he'd been electrocuted.

"Oh, and are you going to that thing tonight?"
Evie asked.

"What thing?"

"The PTA thing."

I groaned. "Aww. Is there a PTA thing?"

"Yep. You going?"

I shrugged. "She hasn't mentioned it, but
probably."

"Yeah, same here," said Evie.
Her smile lit up her whole face.
"See you there!"

CHAPTER 10

THE PTA THING

I slumped in a chair at the back of the class, doing my best to become invisible. Sadly it wasn't working. Mum could clearly still see me.

"Next slide, please, Dylan."

She was standing in front of a scabby pull-down screen in a classroom I hadn't even known existed. Most of the rooms had interactive smartboards but this one had a wonky screen and an ancient projector with all the controls labelled in what I guessed was Russian.

Tonight was Mum's last chance to impress the rest of the PTA. After she and Mrs Green had made their speeches, everyone would be casting their vote to choose the new chair. As far as I was concerned, it couldn't come soon enough.

I tapped the right arrow key on my laptop and the image on screen changed to show a picture of Mum standing outside the school and pointing at it.

"The school," said Mum. She pointed down to the floor at her feet. "This school. And that's me there."

There were eleven other members of the PTA in the room – not counting Mrs Green, who sat at the side with Evie. Their reactions to Mum's slides had started off positively with lots of nodding and murmurs of interest.

Now, though, they all shifted in their seats, looking bored. I couldn't blame them. Mum's slideshow mostly featured selfies of her pointing at things, with no real explanation as to why.

"Next slide, Dylan," said Mum.

I tapped the key on the laptop. The picture changed to show Mum standing in the road outside the school and pointing to a hole in the tarmac.

"Potholes. They need filling in," said Mum. "Next."

I clicked again. This time, a picture of Dad filled the screen. He was topless and sunburned, and wearing a sombrero. The audience sniggered in surprise.

"What's that doing there?" asked Mum, flustered. "Dylan, move on!"

I clicked again. The next slide showed Mum in the street again. This time she was pointing to a car and looking annoyed.

Mum (the real one, not the photo) tutted several times. "And look at this. Look what we have here. A car abandoned in the 'no parking' zone outside the gates, where it's an inconvenience to parents and – yes, I'm going to say it – a *danger* to children. This sort of thing *must* be stopped," she said. "I mean, what sort of person…? Does anyone know whose car this is?"

At the side of the room, Mrs Green let out an irritated sigh. "You know full well whose car it is, Claire. It's mine."

Mum put a hand to her chest and gasped. "Yours? That's *your* car, Helen? Parked on the yellow lines?"

"I was literally there for thirty seconds," Mrs Green protested.

"Forty-four seconds, actually," said Mum.

Mrs Green stood up. "You *timed* me?"

"Don't, Mum," said Evie, but Mrs Green was already thundering across the classroom.

The rest of the PTA – a mix of parents, grandparents, and one woman so old she could only have been a great-great-grandparent –

watched like spectators at a tennis match, their heads tick-tocking left to right between Mum and Mrs Green. The previous chair, who should probably have intervened, also just watched.

"Yes, I timed you," said Mum. "Do you know how many accidents can happen in forty-four seconds, Helen?"

"None!"

"*None?* Don't be ridiculous," Mum spluttered. "A *thousand.*"

Mrs Green's voice got higher and louder. "A thousand? What are you talking about? How could a thousand accidents happen in forty-four seconds?"

That caught Mum off guard. I could tell as soon as she'd said it that she hadn't meant to say "a thousand", and now she was being forced to explain herself. She began listing on her fingers.

"OK, a car could have crashed into the back of

you. A car could have crashed into the side of you. A car could have crashed into the *front* of you."

"It's a one-way street. How could anyone have crashed into the front of me?" Mrs Green demanded.

"They might have been reversing!" said Mum.

Mrs Green gritted her teeth. "*You'll* be reversing in a minute!" she warned. "Right through that wall."

Mum's jaw dropped. She turned to the audience. "Did you hear that? Threats of violence! She *clearly* isn't suited to be chairperson."

"Stop!" I said, standing up. Everyone turned to look at me and I instinctively did the only thing I could. I told the truth. "Look at you both. *Neither* of you are suited to being the chairperson."

"Dylan!" said Mum, looking betrayed.

"Well, it's true! Literally anyone in this room would probably be better than you two," I said. I pointed to the great-great-grandmother. "Even

her, and I'm pretty sure she's either asleep or dead. You've forgotten what the PTA is all about. I mean, I don't know what that is, exactly, but presumably it must have some sort of purpose."

"Beaky's right," said Evie. "And it's not like anyone even cares about the PTA!" She smiled at the rest of the audience. "No offence."

I nodded. "But if, for some *insane* reason, you do care, then you can't vote for either of these two. They don't represent what the PTA stands for – whatever that is. Maybe they did, once, but they've become power-crazed. All they want to do now is beat each other, and they don't care who gets hurt along the way."

"Dylan! That's not true," said Mum.

"Isn't it, Mum? Mrs Green? Can you look me in the eye and honestly tell me you want to be in charge of this lot?"

"No offence," said Evie, smiling at the audience again.

"Or did you just want to win, no matter the cost?"

Mum and Mrs Green looked at each other, then quickly looked away again. They both shuffled their feet.

"You printed two thousand leaflets," I said. "Two *thousand*, and only eleven people here can 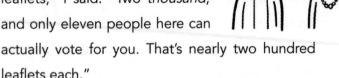 actually vote for you. That's nearly two hundred leaflets each."

"I did *three* thousand," said Mrs Green. She started off sounding quite proud about that but by the end of the sentence just sounded a bit confused.

I knew I was probably going too far now but there was no stopping me. I turned to the rest of the PTA.

"So, when you vote tonight, don't vote for either of these two. Vote for him," I said, pointing to a random man. His eyes went wide with horror and he quickly shook his head. "Or him," I said, gesturing to someone else. I pointed to the ancient woman. "Or her. But ... uh ... seriously, could someone check her pulse? She hasn't moved in, like, twenty minutes."

"She's fine," said Mum.

"She always does that," agreed Mrs Green.

Evie's mum and mine both sighed and started talking at the same time.

"Look, Helen..."

"Claire, I..."

They smiled. "We've been a bit silly, haven't we?" said Mum.

Mrs Green nodded. "A tiny bit," she said. "I'm afraid I got a bit carried away."

"I got more carried away," said Mum.

"Well, I don't know. I got pretty carried away," said Mrs Green.

"Yes, I mean, obviously," agreed Mum. "But what I'm saying is that out of the two of us, *I* was the one who got the *most*—"

"Seriously?" I said. "You're going to argue about this now?"

Both mums looked at each other and laughed.

"Oh, I'm sorry, Helen," said Mum.

"Me, too, Claire," said Mrs Green, and they reached over to give each other a hug.

The outgoing chairperson began to applaud. One other person joined in but it didn't really come to much, and lapsed into a slightly embarrassing silence.

Evie bumped her shoulder against mine. "That was pretty cool, Beaky."

"You were pretty cool yourself," I said, then I felt a hot prickling on my cheeks as I blushed.

Luckily the outgoing chairperson chose that moment to take charge, saving me from saying anything else.

"OK, let's have the vote, shall we?" she said, clapping her hands together. She looked at Mum and Mrs Green. "Are you both still going to stand for the position?"

"Helen, how about we stand together as joint chair?" Mum suggested.

"I'd be honoured to," said Mrs Green. She linked arms with Mum and they both laughed again. It was getting a bit grating, to be honest. "Let the voting begin!"

Ten minutes later I stood in the corridor with Evie, Mum and Mrs Green. Both mums looked a little shell-shocked.

"Well, that was a surprise, wasn't it?" said Mum.

"Yep. I did *not* see that coming," agreed Mrs Green.

The wide-eyed man I'd pointed to during my speech stomped out of the classroom, struggling to carry four boxes of paperwork. He glared at me as he stormed past.

"Thanks a lot, kid," he said.

We all watched him thunder along the corridor. "You'd think he'd be happier that so many people wrote his name on the voting slip," said Mum.

"Yeah," said Mrs Green thoughtfully. "Mind you … it is quite a lot of paperwork, isn't it?"

"True," said Mum, nodding slowly. "And then all the extra meetings with the teachers and the council and what have you. Do you get the feeling, Helen, that we might have dodged a bullet?" asked Mum.

Arm in arm, they strolled along the corridor towards the exit. "Do you know, Claire, I think we just might have."

Evie and I followed behind. "That worked out pretty well," she said. "Our mums are friends again, we don't have to do any more stupid PTA stuff…"

"That old woman's not dead," I added.

"Yeah, that's a bonus," Evie said. She grinned excitedly. "TV thing tomorrow!"

"Yep. TV thing tomorrow."

"Got your cunning plan all figured out?"

"I'd love to say, 'yes', but I'd be lying," I told her. "It's … a work in progress."

"You realize that if you win, I'm going to blackmail you into giving me half the money," Evie said, grinning.

"Half!"

"The price of silence, my friend. The price of silence."

I shrugged. "Fair enough. But let's be honest, neither of us are going to win, anyway."

"I know!" said Evie. "A wasp that ties knots!"

"Mental," I said.

Evie shoulder-bumped me again. "Between the TV thing, hanging out afterwards and the play on Friday, I guess we're going to be seeing a lot of each other over the next few days."

"Yeah," I said reaching for my gobstopper, in case the conversation took an awkward turn. "I guess we are."

CHAPTER 11

TV DAY

I was halfway through a bowl of cereal when Dad slid a shiny disc across the dining table to me. I eyed it with suspicion as I slurped the milk from my spoon.

"What's that?" I asked.

"It's a CD."

"What?"

"A CD. You know, it's got music on it," Dad said.

"No, I mean what's it for? Why are you giving it to me?"

"It's my theme tune for the telly people," Dad

explained. "I thought you could give it to the producer."

"Yeah, I'm not going to do that," I said, sliding the disc back to him.

Dad deflected it back towards me. "Go on. It's good."

I returned the CD. "They've already got a theme tune."

"This one's better," said Dad. The disc came back to my side of the table. I gazed down at it for a little while, before coming to a decision.

"OK, I'll take it," I said.

"And you'll give it to the producer?" Dad said.

Argh! He'd seen through my carefully selected choice of words.

"Definitely not," I said.

"Morning!" trilled Mum, bustling through the front door with such a burst of enthusiasm that Dad and I both jumped in our seats.

She was dressed in tight Lycra leggings and a baggy T-shirt. The T-shirt was an eye-watering shade of orange, with "Ready, Steady ... Fun!" printed on the front in an even more painful shade of lime green.

"I've been running," Mum announced. "Helen and I decided to go for a morning jog. It's time we started looking after ourselves, getting more exercise, cutting down on unhealthy food..."

Jodie leaned her head out from the kitchen. "I've got some bacon on, Mum. Want some?"

"Ooh, yes, please!" said Mum. "And stick a couple of sausages on while you're at it, will you? And tea. Two sugars. Thanks, love."

Jodie rolled her eyes. "Wish I'd never offered," she muttered.

Mum pulled out a chair and sat down next to me.

"You smell," I told her.

"Thanks for that, Dylan," said Mum, but her

smile didn't falter. "I was talking to Helen earlier..."

"What were you saying?" I asked. "Was it, 'Please slow down'?"

"No..."

"Was it, 'I've got to stop or I'll be sick'?"

"No!" said Mum. "We were saying how nice it is that you and Evie are—"

"She's not my girlfriend!" I cried. My gobstopper was upstairs, so I settled for quickly cramming five spoonfuls of Coco Pops into my mouth.

Mum and Dad swapped smiles across the table.

"Whatever you say, sweetheart," Mum said. "Oh, and did I hear right? There's going to be a wasp that ties knots on the TV pet thing?"

I nodded, forcing more cereal into my gob.

"Wait. A wasp?" said Dad. "Someone's got a pet *wasp*?"

I nodded again, making a little bit of chocolatey milk dribble down my chin.

With a sigh, Dad reached across

the table and picked up his CD. "Oh dear. Back to the drawing board," he said. "Verse four is a bit … *anti-insect.*"

"I can't remember, did you actually tell us?" said Mum. "What *is* Destructo's talent?"

"Eating. Got to be eating," said Dad.

"You'd think so, wouldn't you?" I slurred through my mouthful of mushed-up cereal. "That would've made total sense. But, well, I told them he could—"

Before I could finish the sentence, there was a shout from the kitchen. "Destructo! Don't you dare!"

The dog bounded out of the kitchen, a string of sausages trailing behind him. He shot across the room like a furry bullet, just as Jodie emerged from the kitchen waving a wooden spoon.

"Get back here!" she called after him, but Destructo was already halfway up the stairs. If past performances were anything to go by, the sausages would already be gone.

"Yep," I mumbled. "Definitely should've gone with eating."

We had play rehearsals for most of the day, so school passed quite quickly. At least, those bits of it where Wayne wasn't bombarding me with questions about *TV's Most Talented Pets* and his role in the plan.

I was excited about the TV show but nervous at the same time. If everything went according to plan, Destructo would appear to ride my bike. If

it didn't go according to plan, I'd probably be arrested for attempted fraud.

Or disqualified from the competition, at least.

Still, if the whole thing *was* a complete disaster, they'd probably just edit me out of the finished episode.

Or so I thought.

"*Live?* What do you mean *live*?"

Theo shrugged. Rehearsals had finished and we were heading for the school gates a full twelve minutes before the bell rang. "It's broadcast live. It said so on the listings thing on my telly. Today's episode has got your name on it and everything."

"But what if my plan doesn't work? I'll look stupid!" I shook my head emphatically. "No. It can't go out live."

"Well, it is," said Theo. "Good luck convincing them to change it."

"Wait up!" called Wayne, jogging after us. He was struggling to carry a box that was roughly the size of a washing machine.

"Did you get it?" Theo asked him.

"Of course I got it. What do you think this is?" Wayne hissed.

Theo reacted as if he was only just seeing the box for the first time. "Oh right. Yeah."

"Did you take all the alien stuff off it?" I asked.

"It looks just like a dog," Wayne confirmed. "But if anyone gets too close, they'll spot it's a costume right away."

"Leave that bit to us," I said. "Just be in position at 5 p.m., like we planned. And don't forget your bike."

"I'm not an idiot," said Wayne. "See you losers later."

Once he'd gone, Theo made a confession. "Beaky, I'm not sure I can do this."

"What? But you've got to!"

"What if I get caught fiddling with the laptop?" said Theo. "I could get into big trouble."

"You won't get caught," I said. "I'll cause a distraction."

"It'd better be a big one," Theo said.

I grinned. "Oh, trust me. It will be."

CHAPTER 12

THE DISTRACTION

The church hall was busier than I had ever seen it. Mind you, it was only the second time I'd ever set foot in the place, so that wasn't saying much.

It was an ancient wooden building with windows that had been painted shut and some worrying black stains on the ceiling. Destructo and I had been shown to the "Green Room" when we'd arrived, but it was really just a tiny kitchen with a folding table in the corner and a jug of weak orange squash. The lights flickered whenever anyone walked beneath them, so I hadn't hung around in there in case the dodgy electrics zapped me on the head like a bolt of lightning.

There were seven people from the TV company in the main hall, all busily doing stuff in a way that suggested it was very important. A woman said, "One ... one, two," into a big furry microphone. A wiry-looking man positioned lights around a green-screen set that had been put together at the far end of the hall. Another woman with a spiky white Mohican put make-up on the only person I recognized – the presenter, Howard Howard (not his real name, I'm guessing).

Theo was lurking in the corner, watching everyone and occasionally glancing at a laptop set up in front of a row of monitors.

Sebastian Farrinton from Foxley Hill School was already perched on one of the four stools that had been placed on the show's set – three on the left and one on the right. Sebastian was sitting in the middle of the group of three, leaving a space for Evie and me on either side of him. He had a glass jar in one hand and a long piece of string in the other, and he was smirking as if his victory was already in the bag.

"Watch out, coming through," said a cameraman, wheeling his camera past us. Destructo eyed the little wheels on the base of the tripod hungrily.

"Don't you dare," I whispered, tightening my grip on his lead. For all the good that would do me if he decided to run. Even if I could stand my ground, he'd probably rip my arm right off.

I glanced up at the hall's clock and let out a little yelp of panic. There were fewer than forty minutes until the show started, which meant we were running out of time to put my plan into action. I looked over to where Theo was standing and he gestured with his eyes towards the laptop.

I nodded and raised my eyebrows. He looked worried but nodded back. I took a deep breath. This was it, then. It was now or never.

I'd have liked to be sneaky about my distraction but my need to tell the truth didn't let me.

"Just letting Destructo off his lead," I announced. Luckily no one paid me any attention. I unfastened the metal clip. Destructo looked up at me, his tongue hanging out. "And now I'm bouncing this rubber ball, which will make him go nuts."

I hurled the little bouncy ball at the hall floor with all my might. It *boinged* up, ricocheted off the camera, then went flying off towards the show's set. Barking excitedly, Destructo tore after it, barging aside the cameraman, the sound woman and a teenager whose entire job seemed to involve carrying cups of coffee around and getting shouted at.

"Sorry, my fault! I threw that on purpose!" I announced, despite all my best efforts not to. But no one heard me over the shouts and barks and crashing of equipment as Destructo powered across the hall, knocking over everything in his path.

The woman doing the make-up was thrown on to Howard Howard, smearing mascara across his forehead.

"You blithering idiot!" he roared, sounding nothing like the warm and friendly chap he always seemed to be on TV.

As the set collapsed like dominoes, I glanced over to see Theo frantically typing on the laptop's keyboard. He stopped every few seconds to take photos of the screen, and to make sure no one was about to catch him.

After almost a minute of tapping and snapping, he backed away and gave me a thumbs up, then sidled towards the door.

By this point, half of the equipment in the hall had been knocked over, two thirds of the production crew were shouting as they tried to catch falling bits of the set, and Sebastian Farrinton was standing on his stool, clutching the jar to his chest.

"G-get away!" he wailed, even though Destructo was paying him no attention whatsoever. "Get away, you *brute*!"

Destructo let out a happy yelp as he finally caught the ball, then chewed it twice before swallowing it. He trotted back towards me, licking his chops and looking really quite pleased with himself.

I clipped him back on his lead and looked up to find every single person in the room staring at me in mute disbelief.

I smiled sheepishly. "Dogs, eh?" I said, then I about-turned and let Destructo drag me towards the door. "It's probably best if I take him outside. Just shout when you're ready for us."

With Destructo leading the way, we ran out into the car park to find Theo sitting with his back to the wall, writing on a big piece of card with a Sharpie.

"Did you get it?" I asked.

Theo nodded and held up his phone. "Got it. Photographed the whole script."

"Brilliant!" I cheered. "Now you can write a load of lies about Destructo and the bike, I'll be able to read them, and no one will be any the wiser."

"Any the wiser about what?"

I turned to find Evie standing right behind me, her cat Gizmo in her arms. Destructo shot the cat a wary glance, then tucked himself in behind me. Despite being the size of a lion, he'd been scared of cats ever since one had roughed him up in an alleyway when he was a puppy.

Gizmo shot him a look that seemed to say, "I'm watching you, sunshine," then went back to licking her paws.

"About Theo feeding me the answers to

Howard's questions, and Wayne dressing up as Destructo," I blurted, then I smiled and waved. "Hi."

"Oh, *that*," said Evie. "Hi yourself." She nodded towards the door. "Should we go in?"

"I'd maybe give it a minute," I said. "Destructo kind of wrecked … well, everything, really. They're probably still a bit angry."

"Aaargh! That *stupid* dog!" snapped a voice from inside the hall.

"OK, a *lot* angry," I said.

"Oh! I forgot! I saw Wayne," said Evie. "He says he can't make it."

My heart somersaulted into my throat. "What?"

"Just kidding," Evie giggled. "He said to tell you he's in position and ready when you are."

"Thank goodness for that," I wheezed, clutching at my chest.

Evie shuffled on the spot for a bit, obviously building up to something. "So ... still on for hanging out after this?"

The squeaking of Theo's Sharpie stopped. I didn't dare turn to look at him. "Um ... yeah. Yep. Still on for ... that. What you said."

"Cool," Evie said.

"Right," I said. "Cool."

The teenager whose job it was to get coffee and be shouted at appeared in the doorway. "Uh, Dylan and ... are you Evie?"

"That's me," said Evie.

"Great. I need you both to come inside with your pets, so you can get your mics on."

Theo's Sharpie started squeaking again, faster than ever.

"OK, then!" I puffed out my cheeks and shot Evie a worried smile. "Looks like it's show time!"

CHAPTER 13

SHOW TIME

Over the course of the next twenty minutes, Evie and I were introduced to everyone involved in the show. Despite Destructo's rampage earlier, everyone seemed pretty nice, with the exception of Howard Howard, who – from what I could tell – hated everyone.

The only person in the room who was even more unpleasant than the show's presenter was Sebastian, the Foxley Hill kid. Whenever Evie or I tried to speak to him his nostrils flared like he'd detected a bad smell and he started babbling baby talk to the jar with his wasp in it.

"Where's my wittle Gavin? Where's my ittle wittle Gavin?"

"Why did you call him Gavin?" I asked.

Sebastian sighed quite forcibly. "Because he looks like my great-uncle."

"Oh right. So was Gavin your great-uncle's name?" asked Evie.

Sebastian sighed even more violently. "Don't be ridiculous."

Evie and I both exchanged a look, then shrugged. "Bit weird, but fair enough," I said, and we left the conversation there.

Across the hall, Howard Howard batted the make-up woman away and strode over to us. As he took his seat, he shot Destructo a look of such contempt I could have sworn I felt the air *crackle*. Of course, it might just have been the dodgy electrics.

"Hello," said Sebastian, offering a hand to shake.

Howard didn't acknowledge it, and instead just gave the Foxley Hill boy a slow look up and down.

"Are you the wasp one?"

"Uh, yes. I'm Sebastian. This is Gavin." He held up the jar and I got my first proper glimpse of the wasp. It looked just like any other wasp, and I was glad it was currently trapped behind glass.

Howard made no effort to hide his distaste and turned his attention to Evie. Gizmo was still in her arms, peering out suspiciously at all the unfamiliar faces.

Gizmo!

"Are you the drum-cat?"

"Uh, *I'm* not, no. My cat is."

"Ha. Yes," said Howard, very much not laughing. "Quite. And you..." He fixed me with a cold stare. "I'm painfully aware of who you are. Keep that mutt under control."

"I'll do my best," I said.

"OK, quiet on set, everyone," announced

someone from behind the camera. "Going live in fifteen."

Evie, Sebastian and I all shuffled on our stools. Howard Howard leaned in and glared at us all in turn. "Remember, this is going out live to the nation. Millions of people will be watching your every move and listening to your every word. We could well be in line for a *TV Choice Award* this year, so do not mess this up, or so help me God, I will rain down fire upon you all. Is that understood? I will rain down fire upon—!"

"Five, four, three..."

Howard straightened up and fixed the camera with a beaming smile, just as the light above it turned red. "Hello! And welcome to a very special live roadshow edition of *TV's Most Talented Pets*," he said, his voice light and breezy. "I'm Howard Howard, and joining me today are Evie Green and her drum-playing cat, Gizmo!"

The crew applauded as the camera angled slightly to focus on Evie. She held up one of Gizmo's paws and made him wave.

"Haha! Delightful," said Howard Howard. "Say hello to Sebastian Farrinton and his rather *unusual* pet, Gavin, who – wait for it – is a wasp!"

"Hello," said Sebastian, lifting the jar up so the camera could see it.

"Now, Sebastian, I've heard a lot of *buzz* about Gavin, and I for one can't wait to see him in action later," said Howard Howard, and the crew made a valiant attempt at laughter.

"Aaaaand last, but by no means least, it's Dylan Malone and his Great Dane, Destructo."

From my seat, I could see the autocue screen right above the camera lens, where Howard's lines were slowly scrolling. I glanced past the cameraman at the window beyond. On the other

136

side of the glass, Theo was flicking through the pieces of card he'd written my answers on. Luckily I could manage this one by myself.

"All right?" I said.

"And there we have this week's three contestants and their perfectly precocious pets!"

The cameraman moved backwards as a short blast of music rang out from somewhere right behind my head. When it stopped Howard clapped his hands together, then turned to address us all.

"OK, before we get started, a quick question for all three of you. Aside from their talent, what's the *very best thing* about your pets?" he asked. "Evie, coming to you first. What's the best thing about Gizmo?"

"She's always up for playing and having fun. I suppose that's the best thing about… Oh, no wait! Killing stuff."

Howard Howard's face froze. "I'm sorry?"

"A rat got into the kitchen a few months ago and Gizmo killed it."

"Right. I see."

"It was pretty brutal. That's probably her best thing."

"Good, right," said Howard Howard, quickly moving down the line. "Sebastian. What's the best thing about Gavin?"

Sebastian thought for a moment. "Uh, he's got so many good qualities but I suppose if I had to choose … sense of humour."

If Howard had looked surprised at Evie's answer, it was nothing compared to the expression he wore now. He blinked several times in rapid succession, his smile fixed in place. "Sorry, sense of…?"

"Humour," said Sebastian, his face completely straight. "He's funny. Well, I think he is, anyway."

Howard's eyes crept down to the wasp in the jar. "*Do* you? Right. Wonderful. Good. And Dylan?

How about you?"

"I don't know," I said. "I've never met him before."

Howard frowned. "Sorry?"

"The wasp," I said. "I've never met him. I've got no idea if he's funny."

"What? No," said Howard, unable to disguise the irritation in his voice. He laughed falsely. "I mean what's the best thing about Destructo?"

Through the window, Theo fumbled for a card, then held it up. He grinned at me over the top, and I felt my stomach flip.

Oh no.

Oh no, he *hadn't*.

"I love how his breath smells," I said, reading from the card. Theo flipped it over and laughed silently as he pointed

I love how his breath smells

to the words on the other side. "It smells like fairy hiccups."

Howard Howard shot the camera a sideways glance and Theo quickly lowered the card out of sight. "Uh ... right. Great! Well, now that we've got to know our contestants and their pets a little better, it's time to check out their talents. But first, here's a reminder of what our contestants could win."

The light on the camera blinked out. "VT rolling. Back in twenty," chimed a voice from the crew.

"What was all that about?" hissed Howard Howard. "Why are you coming out with rubbish like that?"

I opened my mouth to reply, then realized he was talking to Sebastian. "How can a wasp have a sense of humour? It's a wasp!"

"Yes, but Gavin's special," Sebastian insisted. "When you get to know him, you'll find—"

"But I'm not going to get to know him, am I?" hissed Howard Howard. "He's a wasp. I mean, what sort of weirdo—?"

"And we're back in four, three…"

Howard Howard turned to the camera, his smile clicking on at the same time as the red "On Air" light.

"That's right, five thousand pounds, plus a chance at *twenty-thousand* pounds and – let's not forget – a pat from the queen." Everyone in the room glanced, just briefly, at Sebastian's jar. All of us, I imagine, were trying to picture the queen patting a wasp.

"So!" said Howard Howard, all chirpy and full of fun. "Let's get started!" After a brief chat with Evie, a set of drums was wheeled in.

Evie plonked Gizmo down on the drum kit's padded seat and we all watched and waited as she sniffed the high-hat. Gizmo, I mean, not Evie.

At first the cat just looked a bit confused by the whole thing, but then she stretched herself up on to her back legs and began thudding her paws on the snare drum. *Dum. Dum-dum.*

"Aw," said Howard Howard. "How *wonderful.*"

"She hasn't started yet," said Evie. "She's just testing the sound."

"Oh."

With her sound-check complete, Gizmo bounded up on to the drum kit and began throwing herself around, a thrashing ball of legs and tail, sweeping like a tornado across the drums. By rights, she should have been making a pretty awful racket but somehow her frenzied thrashing and leaping was producing an actual rhythm.

Dum-dum-tsh-tsh, dum-dum-tsh-tsh, badda-badda-badda-badda dum-dum-tish.

I stared. Howard Howard stared. Even Sebastian, whose confidence had seemed pretty rock-solid so far, gave his jar a doubting glance.

Gizmo finished with a flurry of *baddas, dums* and *tshs*, and the crew erupted into cheers and applause.

"Amazing! Wonderful! Dare I say it? *Pet-tastic!*" said Howard Howard, beaming from ear to ear.

Evie took a bow, scooped Gizmo into her arms, then hurried back to her stool.

Howard began to ask her his scripted questions. I didn't really hear them or Evie's responses. I was too busy trying to combat the rising feeling of terror inside me. I could see my name creeping up from the bottom of the screen, which meant he was coming to me next. The big moment had almost arrived.

"Thank you, Evie … and the drum-playing superstar, Gizmo!" said Howard Howard, and another burst of music played, accompanied by applause from the crew.

Howard turned to the camera. "Now, what if I said our next guest is a dog? You'd probably say, 'So what, Howard? It *is* a show about pets, you know!'" He nodded and chuckled. "And you'd be right! But what if I said our next guest is a dog *who can ride a bike*?"

Howard pointed at the camera and smiled. "Ah! That got your attention. Well, say hello to Dylan Malone and his bicycling best buddy, Destructo. Dylan, welcome."

Destructo, who'd been lying beside me on the floor, chose that moment to raise his back leg and begin vigorously licking his bum.

"Hello," I said, trying to ignore the bottom licking.

"So, Dylan. Tell us about Destructo," said Howard, reading from his autocue.

At the window, Theo fumbled with his cards. "When did he first learn to ride a bike?"

"Ages ago," I said, reading from Theo's card.

"Right. I see," said Howard. "Can you be more specific?"

That wasn't on his autocue! At the window, I saw Theo frantically rummaging through his cards. It seemed to take forever before he finally held one up for me to read from.

"No," I said.

Howard Howard hesitated, then his smile returned, wider than ever. "Well then, before we chat any further, let's see him in action. Dylan Malone, the time has come. Show us your pet's special talent!"

CHAPTER 14

DOG FIGHT

A few people had gathered around the edge of the car park to watch. They waved and cheered as Destructo dragged me round the side of the hall, straining on his lead.

Thanks to Theo and his cards, I'd been able to explain to Howard Howard that the cameraman had to keep his distance or Destructo would be too nervous. The cameraman was waiting at the front of the hall, ready to capture the moment when Destructo came cycling round the corner.

Wayne's bike was propped up against the wall

but Wayne himself was nowhere to be seen.

"Psst!" I whispered, covering my clip-on microphone with my hand. "Wayne? Where are you?"

A furry grey head popped up from behind a bush and Destructo let out a low threatening growl.

"Shh, it's just Wayne," I said, tugging on the lead. Destructo stopped growling but kept his eyes fixed firmly on the vaguely dog-shaped figure that clambered out from behind the bushes. "Hurry up!" I urged. "They're waiting."

Wayne was right – up close, the disguise wasn't even a little bit convincing. It looked like someone had tried to make a Scooby-Doo costume and given up halfway through. In the cold light of day it was more brown than grey and the paws were all larger than my head.

"It doesn't have a tail!" I realized.

"Neither does your dog," said Wayne, his voice muffled by the headpiece.

Without a word, I pointed to Destructo's tail.

"Oh, right," said Wayne, straining to look down. "Has he always had that?"

"Just get on the bike!" I hissed.

While Wayne clambered on, I peeked round the side of the hall. The camera was pointed my way and Howard Howard stood in front of it, presumably filling time until Destructo emerged.

I gave them a thumbs up, then ducked back out of sight. Wayne was perched on the bike but his massive paws were making it hard to get his feet on the pedals.

"I can't see very well," he said.

Destructo growled again and I gave another tug on the lead. "Just go in a straight line, then turn and come back," I urged. "That's all you have to do."

"Right," said Wayne. "Here I go!"

With a few turns of the pedals, Wayne went wobbling out from behind the church hall. I peeked round the corner to see Howard turning to watch. He had a look of genuine wonder and amazement on his face and right then – for that brief, glorious moment – I thought the plan was actually going to work.

And then Destructo started to chase the bike, and that's where it all went wrong.

He shot after it like a cheetah after ... whatever it is that cheetahs chase. Giraffes, maybe? I tried to hold on to his lead but he dragged me into the car park and I knew that if I wanted to keep my arm, I'd have to release my grip.

Free of me holding him back, Destructo ran faster. Hearing the barking behind him, Wayne pedalled harder. Even through the costume, I could hear his muffled cries for help as Destructo tore after him, snapping and snarling.

"Get off! Beaky! Heeeeelp!"

Wayne lurched to the left and was now racing straight for the ramshackle old fence at the side of the car park. The onlookers screamed and scattered as Wayne and Destructo barrelled straight towards them.

I – along with millions of people at home – watched, transfixed, as the front wheel of the bike hit the fence and Wayne was launched over the handlebars and landed with a *thump* in a patch of waste ground on the other side.

Destructo wasn't letting him get away that easily, though. He vaulted the fence in a single bound. There was a growling, followed by a tearing, followed by a screaming. Wayne jumped to his feet, now missing the costume's head, and ran for his life, sobbing and crying.

I turned to find Howard glaring at me. The camera was still watching Wayne, and Howard's face was red with fury. He pointed to me, then jabbed a thumb towards the door of the church hall before turning and marching inside.

For a split second, I thought about running away. I could join the circus. Or just hide under my bed. Anything that meant I didn't have to go back in there.

But I knew I couldn't do that. I had to see this through. Besides, it wasn't like things could really get any worse.

Destructo trotted up to me, a bit of greyish-brown fabric hanging from his jaws.

I sighed and took hold of his lead. "Come on," I said. "We'd better go and face the music."

CHAPTER 15

THE BOMBSHELL

As I sat back down, I expected everyone to start shouting at me but to my amazement, they pretty much carried on as usual.

Rather than angrily accuse me of cheating, which is what I'd expected to happen, they just sort of laughed it off and pretended the demonstration had gone a bit wrong. I suppose they had to do that, what with it being a live broadcast and everything. They couldn't exactly pin me in a corner and beat me up, or risk shouting at me so much I burst into tears.

The only problem was, because the demonstration hadn't gone as expected, Howard was no longer working from his autocue, and was improvising his questions to me, which meant Theo's cards were useless.

"So, Dylan, what went wrong there?" Howard asked.

I glanced out of the window at Theo, who was frantically flicking through his cards, trying to find one to fit the bill. "Quite a lot," I said, stalling for time.

"Haha! Yes, you can say that again," said Howard, winking to the camera. "But specifically, where do you think the problem lay?"

Theo shrugged and held up a card. I read it. "My dog can ride a bike."

"Uh, yes. We saw... Well, I'm not sure what we saw, exactly, but..."

"It smells like fairy hiccups," I said, reading from another of Theo's cards that flashed up. Theo pulled a horrified face and shook his head. "No, wait, I didn't mean that," I said. "That's the one from earlier."

Theo pulled the top card away but that just revealed the one below.

"Hooray, I've won!" I read.

"Er, no. You haven't," said Howard Howard.

Theo turned his stack of cards round. Unfortunately, this revealed another answer. "Sometimes he poos on the table."

Theo tossed all the cards to the ground, where I couldn't see them. By then, though, the damage was done. Everyone was staring at me, even Destructo.

I cleared my throat quietly. "Don't really know why I kept reading those," I said. "Should have just stopped talking."

Howard Howard stared at me in confusion. Evie

154

reached behind the back of the stools and tapped me on the side. "You OK?" she somehow managed to ask using just her eyebrows.

The look between us didn't go unnoticed. Howard Howard smiled and turned his attention back to the autocue. I glanced at the words scrolling up the screen and felt my blood run cold.

"Leaving the pets aside for a moment, a little birdie tells me that we may have our very own *TV's Most Talented Pets* romance brewing, right here in the studio."

"It's not a studio, it's a manky old church hall," I said, quickly trying to change the subject.

"Haha! Yes, quite," said Howard Howard, smiling through his obvious rage.

Evie looked across at me in surprise but I didn't dare meet her gaze. Instead I just watched in slowly dawning horror as the text continued up the autocue display.

Theo had his arms folded and was leaning

against the outside window ledge, smirking at me with his face right up to the glass. The words on the autocue were all written in lower case and littered with spelling mistakes. It didn't take a genius to work out who was responsible.

Theo!

"So what I want to know," said Howard Howard, frowning slightly as he struggled to read the typo-filled text. "Is, does Beaky want Evie to be his girlfriend or what?"

The presenter's frown deepened. "Who's Beaky?" he asked.

"That's me," I croaked. I shoved my hand into my pocket, grabbing for my gobstopper, only to find it gone. Outside, Theo held up the bag with the big sweet inside and flashed me a grin.

"Oh no," I whispered, feeling the eyes of the nation boring into me down the camera lens. "Not now. Not like this! Not on live TV!"

Evie's face was red but she was smiling. Sebastian

sat between us, cradling his wasp jar and looking increasingly impatient.

Howard Howard raised his perfectly plucked eyebrows. "Well, Dylan?" he asked. "I know that I, for one, can't wait to hear the answer! Would you like Evie to be your girlfriend?"

As I sat there on my stool, Evie blushing nearby, Theo laughing on the other side of the window and a million-plus people watching at home, I couldn't keep the truth inside any longer. It rose like a bubble all the way up my windpipe, before bursting on my lips like an explosion of pure humiliation.

"No," I said. "I wouldn't."

Well, I never said it was *me* the gobstopper was saving from being humiliated, did I?

I shot Evie an apologetic look but her face sort of crumpled and she looked away.

NO, I WOULDN'T

157

Theo looked in through the window, his mouth hanging open. Clearly he hadn't been expecting that answer.

"I'm sorry, Evie," I said.

But she just stared straight ahead and patted Gizmo's head so forcefully the poor cat's eyes went as wide as saucers of milk.

"Is it my turn yet?" demanded Sebastian. "Gavin's going to need a nap soon, if we don't hurry up."

"What?" said Howard Howard. Even *he* looked like he felt sorry for Evie, which was saying something. He blinked and shook his head. "Um, yes. Yes! It's… Next up is … the, uh, kid with the bee."

"Wasp," tutted Sebastian.

"Yes, right. Wasp," said Howard. "The kid with the pet wasp who can play the… No, wait! Knots, wasn't it?"

Evie stood up suddenly. Howard Howard turned

to speak to her but she barged past him and ran off the set. A moment later, the church hall shook as she slammed the door.

The lights all flickered, then something in the camera went *bang*, sending a puff of dark smoke drifting up towards the ceiling.

"Equipment's all down," cried someone from the crew. "We're off air."

I slapped my hands on my thighs and did my best to smile. "Still, do you know what?" I said to the room in general. "This wasn't as bad as I expected."

The fire alarm began to screech. A moment later, the overhead sprinklers activated, showering us all in freezing-cold water.

"OK," I muttered, as everyone screamed and Destructo started barking his head off. "*Now* it's as bad as I expected."

WOOF!

BARK! WOOF!

CHAPTER 16

AFTERSHOCKS

After the show – which, to my surprise, the coffee-fetching teenager assured me was only the *second* worst episode ever – I met Theo outside. His chewed his lip guiltily.

"I thought you'd say 'yes'!" he said. "I thought it'd be funny if you owned up to fancying Evie on the telly. I thought that's why you kept shoving in the gobstopper, so you didn't embarrass yourself by admitting it."

I sighed and shook my head. "No. It was so I didn't embarrass her by denying it," I said, squirming a bit. "She's my friend. I didn't want to hurt her feelings."

We both looked in the direction Evie had run off in. "I think you might have hurt her feelings," Theo said.

"Oh, you think so?" I said, then I shook my head. There was no point worrying about it now. "Come on, we'd better go and find Wayne."

We eventually found him up in the branches of a tree. It turns out that Wayne is less scared of heights than he is of big angry dogs trying to eat him.

Not that Destructo would have actually eaten him, of course. He'd just have eaten the costume and left Wayne to run home in his pants.

"Keep it away!" he howled. "That dog's mental."

"Yeah," I admitted. "He is a bit. I've got him now, though. You can come down."

"No chance!" Wayne spluttered. "I'm staying up here until it's gone."

Theo leaned Wayne's bike against the tree and hung the costume's head over the handlebars. "I'll just leave this here, then," he said.

"OK, just get the dog away!" Wayne wailed.

"Come on, Destructo," I said, tugging on the lead.

Destructo fired another couple of barks in Wayne's direction, then turned and began dragging me along the pavement.

"Did we win?" Wayne shouted after us.

"No. Sorry."

"You mean I did all this for *nothing*?"

"Pretty much," I said. "If it's any consolation, we didn't technically lose, either. They called the whole thing off and made us promise never to speak of it again."

Leaving Wayne to make his own way down, Theo and I headed for home. As we reached his front gate, I braced myself against a lamp post to stop Destructo dragging me on.

"Look, Beaky, about the Evie thing," Theo said. "I honestly didn't mean it to go like that. You should have told me."

"Yeah. I know," I said.

"I thought you liked her."

"I do. As a friend. That's why I didn't want to embarrass her," I said. I shot Theo a meaningful look. "And *especially* not on live television."

"Yeah. Sorry," Theo said. He rummaged in his pocket, then held out the gobstopper bag. I took it without a word and stuck it in my trouser pocket.

"Think she's OK?" Theo asked.

"I don't know," I said. "I'll try to talk to her tomorrow."

I looked along the street in the direction of my house. "But right now, I'd better go home and see what Mum and Dad have to say."

Theo smiled in sympathy. "It might not be too bad," he said. "Who knows? Maybe they weren't even watching."

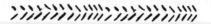

"Bravo! Bravo! What a performance!" said Jodie, standing up and applauding as I shuffled in through the front door. "I mean … I have *genuinely* never seen anything quite like that on TV before. The nonsensical answers, Destructo chasing a boy in a dog suit and then, as if that wasn't enough, everything blows up!"

"Yeah, yeah. Shut up," I said. "Did Mum and Dad see?"

"See what?" asked Mum's voice from the kitchen. She and Dad emerged, looking ashen-faced. "You trying to commit fraud? You making a fool of poor Evie Green on live television? Yes, Dylan. We saw.

I mean … Destructo riding a bike? What were you thinking?"

"I can explain," I said, but Dad shook his head. For once, he looked almost as angry as Mum.

"Not tonight, Dylan. We don't want to hear it," he said. "I think you should probably just go to bed."

"But—"

"Bed," said Mum. "Now."

ZZzZzZZZ

Mum and Dad still weren't up for talking about the TV disaster at breakfast the next morning. I ate in silence, then hid in my room until it was time to go to school.

As I hurried through the school corridors, pretty much everyone was either a) staring at me, b) laughing at me, or c) both. I kept my eyes open for

Evie but when I did finally spot her, Chloe blocked my path.

"Aaaand where do you think *you're* going?" Chloe demanded.

"I want to talk to Evie," I said. "I want to explain."

"Well, you can't," Chloe told me. "You've done enough damage. Also..."

She thumped me on the arm with a surprising amount of force.

"Ow!"

"You totally had that coming," Chloe said. She raised a carefully manicured finger and pointed it in my face. "Stay away from Evie. She doesn't want to talk to you."

The bell rang before I could argue. I watched, glumly, as Chloe linked arms with Evie and led her away.

Maybe it was for the best. I'd completely humiliated Evie on live television. Maybe I *shouldn't* ever talk to her again.

Of course, there was one big flaw in that plan. Tonight was the school play. I was going to have to stand up in the school hall and confess my undying love for her.

Still, I thought, as I trudged off towards class. *At least we haven't sold many tickets.*

"A full house? What do you mean a full house?" I spluttered.

Ms Brannan nodded excitedly. "I know! Isn't it *brilliant*! We completely sold out after your and Evie's TV thing yesterday," she said. "Romeonulan and Julietraxis together before the nation – what better advertising could we have had?" She raised her eyebrows. "How did that go, by the way? I didn't get to watch it."

"Terrible," I said. "But this is even *worse*. How can it have sold out?"

"Well … because people bought all the tickets,"

said Ms Brannan slowly, in case she lost me somewhere. "We had four hundred tickets and now we have none."

"Four *hundred* people are coming?" I yelped.

"Actually more like five hundred," she said. "We had some set aside for parents and staff. It'll be standing room only at the back!"

I slumped down on to a chair that had been decorated to look like an alien throne. "This is bad," I mumbled. "This is really bad."

"Don't be a silly Dylly," said Ms Brannan. "This is what we wanted. A big audience, all here to see you and…" She frowned and glanced around. "Where *is* Evie, by the way? Have you seen her?"

"Seen her? Yes. Spoken to her? No," I said.

"I hope she gets here soon," said Ms Brannan. "It's less than an hour until curtain up, and we still have to rehearse the kiss."

I felt my mouth flop open. "Rehearse the what?" I croaked.

"The kiss. I've decided we should end Scene Twelve with a kiss. It'll be very romantic."

I put my head in both hands. "You can't! No way! Uh-uh. Not on my watch! *Have you lost your mind?*"

"Calm down, Dylan!" said Ms Brannan, taken aback. "It's a stage kiss. Just a peck. It'll bring the house down." She winked. "Besides I heard there might be a real Romeonulan and Julietraxis romance going on between you two!"

"You really didn't watch the TV show, did you?" I groaned but before I could say any more, Ms Brannan pushed past me.

"Wayne!" she gasped. "What on Earth happened to that costume?"

Wayne had been tiptoeing across the stage, dragging the torn and filthy dog costume behind him. He froze when the teacher spotted him, then looked down at the outfit as if he hadn't noticed he was holding it.

"Huh. I don't know, Miss," he said. "I found it like this. It looks like it's been damaged in some way. I wonder how that could have happened?"

Ms Brannan waved a hand. "No time to worry about how, just take it to Chloe and see if she can do something with it. We can't very well do the play without our Astrohound, can we?"

Wayne's face lit up. "Chloe? Brilliant!" Then he cleared his throat and reined in his delight. "I mean … right, I'll go and see her now, Miss."

The next forty minutes passed very slowly. I wriggled into my ridiculous alien-Romeo costume, complete with its four fake arms. Theo turned up, switched on every single one of the lights, then came backstage. Even through the thick stage curtains I could hear the clattering of chairs that told me the hall was filling up.

"Pretty big audience out there," Theo said. "I think quite a lot of them saw you on telly."

I sighed. "This is going to be awful."

"Yeah, probably," Theo admitted.

"And there's no sign of Evie," I said. "What if she doesn't turn up?"

Theo looked past me. "Um…"

"Uh. Hi."

I turned – in quite an undignified way, thanks to the costume – to find Evie standing behind me. "Evie! Hi!" I said, far too enthusiastically.

Evie's own enthusiasm was at the opposite end of the scale. Her face wasn't really showing any emotion at all, although it was quite hard to tell with her purple face paint on. "Can I talk to you?"

"What? Yes, of course!" I said.

We both looked at Theo, who raised his eyebrows and smiled back at us.

"We want you to go away," I said.

"Oh, right. Gotcha!" said Theo, sidling off.

"Evie, about yesterday—" I began, but she cut me off.

"No, don't say anything," she said. "I've been thinking about it a lot, and … obviously someone messed with the autocue thing and, well, I have to know. Was it a joke? Did you think it would be funny to embarrass me?"

"What? No!" I told her. "I wasn't joking."

"Right," she breathed, and for a moment she looked relieved.

"I was telling the truth," I continued. "I really *don't* want to be your boyfriend."

Evie's face did that tissue-crumple thing.

"No, I don't mean it like that!" I said, but she cut me off again.

"No, it's fine. Please ... don't. Let's just do the stupid play."

"Right. Yeah," I said, nodding. "Maybe we can talk afterwards?"

Evie shook her head and backed away. "No. Let's not."

"But Evie!"

She smiled but it wasn't a real smile. It wasn't even close. "Just leave it, Dylan, OK?"

Dylan? She never called me Dylan. This was worse than I thought.

Ms Brannan came up to me and we both watched Evie go. "I asked her about the kiss," she said. "She didn't seem keen."

"Really?" I said. "You don't say."

CHAPTER 17
THE PLAY'S THE THING

We were fifteen minutes into *Romeo and Juliet …
But With Aliens* and it was already worse than I'd
feared. And believe me, I feared it was going to be
terrible.

Theo had been true to his word and turned the
lights up to full power so whenever anyone stepped

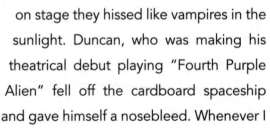

on stage they hissed like vampires in the
sunlight. Duncan, who was making his
theatrical debut playing "Fourth Purple
Alien" fell off the cardboard spaceship
and gave himself a nosebleed. Whenever I

stepped out from the wings, most of my lines were drowned out by the kids in the audience laughing, jeering and singing "Who Let the Dogs Out" and Mr Lawson had to interrupt my second scene and come out on stage to shout at everyone to shut up.

There were a few smaller problems, too. One of my arms fell off (a fake one, thankfully). And Duggie, the kid who was supposed to be wearing the alien dog costume, didn't turn up, so Wayne had to do it instead.

I suppose it could have been worse. Having learned his lesson yesterday, Theo was on the ball with my lines. He got all the cards in the right order and only one of them was upside down. Everyone else fumbled and mumbled through their lines, and Evie, who had been brilliant in rehearsals, looked like she'd rather be anywhere else.

But it was all plodding along and there were

only a few scenes left. I just had to read a dozen or so more lines, then I could go home, hide in the shed and never show my face in public again. It was a foolproof plan.

"OK, Scene Twelve," whispered Ms Brannan, shoving me on stage from the wings. "Go, go, go."

I stumbled out with a "Waargh!", which amused the audience no end. Evie was already on stage, shielding her eyes from Theo's retina-melting lighting. Theo himself stood in the wings across from me, the next card already in position.

Someone wolf-whistled from the audience and a few of the older kids laughed. Mr Lawson half stood up from his seat, gave a loud *Shhh* then sat down again.

With a quick sideways glance to the audience, Evie began to recite her lines.

"Wilt thou be gone? It is not yet near day.

It was the astrobird and not the starlark,

That pierc'd the fearful hollow of thine ear;

Nightly she sings on yond smoogontonk tree.

Believe me, love, it was the astrobird."

I stared at her. Like pretty much every line in the play, I had absolutely no idea what any of that meant. I know Ms Brannan had added some alien stuff to it but the whole thing might as well have been in Martian as far as I was concerned.

Theo raised the card with my scripted response on it. I just had to read it. That was all. I just had to read that card and a few others, and it would all be over. Job done.

And yet...

"Wilt thou be gone? It is not yet near day," Evie began again, a bit louder in case I hadn't heard her the first time.

I glanced again at my cue card. I just had to read the stupid lines. Then the play would be finished and we could go home.

And Evie would never let me talk to her ever again.

She'd never let me tell her the whole truth.

The audience's chuckling fell away to silence. Theo gestured to the card he was holding. I looked from it to Evie, then out over the rest of the hall. That last one almost blinded me, thanks to Theo's lights, but I did my best to ignore the glare as I stepped towards the edge of the stage.

"Hi," I said.

A surprised murmuring went around the audience.

"All right, Beaky?" called someone near the back, and there was another ripple of laughter.

"No, not really," I said. I cupped my hands over my eyes and looked along the front row until I saw Mum and Dad. I gave them a wave and said. "Sorry I told the TV people Destructo could ride a bike."

I raised my eyes to the rest of the hall. "He can't, by the way. That was Wayne in a costume. He's supposed to be wearing it in the next scene, but... Well, I don't know if there'll be a next scene."

There were still a few people laughing but it sounded a bit unsure and awkward now. I waited a few seconds until it faded away, then I took a deep breath.

"My name is Dylan Malone and I cannot tell a lie," I announced. "Don't believe me? Let's see... Here, how about this? If my big sister annoys me, I sneak into her room when she's out and fart on her pillow."

"What!" screeched a voice from near the back of the hall.

I smiled. "Hi, Jodie!"

179

More laughter, but this time not at my expense.

"I'm going to get you for this, Beaky!" Jodie shouted.

"She won't," I said. "Because I've read her diary and know all her secrets." I pointed to a boy in the audience. "She likes your legs, by the way, but thinks your face is a bit like a tomato."

I began counting things off on my fingers. "I regularly wear the same pants for weeks. I sometimes sing into a hairbrush and pretend I'm the lead singer of Queen. If you don't know who they are, ask your dads. It was me who drew that picture of Mr Lawson dressed like Hitler on the bike sheds. Twice."

"I *knew* it!" Mr Lawson cried. "See me on Monday morning."

"Will do, sir."

"I stick bogies under the desk in every class. I once wrote a letter to Santa asking him to turn me into the Incredible Hulk. I use my dad's toothbrush to clean my dog's teeth."

"You do *what*?" Dad yelped.

"The point is, I can't lie," I said. "But I don't always tell the whole truth, either, and sometimes that's even worse."

Evie's eyes widened in horror as I turned to her. "Beaky? What are you doing?" she hissed. "Can we just get on with the play?"

"Evie, I know you'd never give me a chance to explain if I didn't do this now," I said, feeling my cheeks sting red. "The truth is, I think you're amazing. You're funny, you're smart, your eyebrows make you look like a cartoon…"

Her eyebrows met in the middle and I felt the need to clarify. "In a good way, I mean. The truth is, I like you, Evie. I *really* like you."

You could have heard a pin drop. I could feel all eyes on me, burning even more intensely than the lights.

"But it's also true that I don't want you to be my girlfriend." I saw the hurt on her face and quickly explained. "But only because I don't want *anyone* to be my girlfriend. Not yet, anyway. My life's too complicated as it is. Between being shoved in a truth-telling machine, having a dog who tries to eat the TV all the time and, you know, having to put up with my parents…"

"Oi!" protested Dad, but Mum quickly shushed him.

"I'm just not ready for a girlfriend. Not yet," I said. I took a deep breath. "But, well, when I am… Whenever that is, I'd *really* like it to be you."

A series of "oohs" and "awws" went around the audience, accompanied by the occasional sound of someone pretending to throw up. At least, I hope they were pretending.

"So, uh, Evie," I said. "Would you do me the

honour of *not* being my girlfriend?"

Evie was just staring at me with a mixture of horror and confusion. "I'm still at 'cartoon eyebrows'," she said, but then her purple-painted face broke into a smile. "OK, not-boyfriend," she said. "It's a deal."

From out in the audience, someone began to applaud, slow and steady, each clap echoing around the hall. I cupped my hands over my eyes and peered out to see an old woman with hair like a startled scarecrow giving me a standing ovation.

Madame Shirley!

Before I could react, the rest of the audience got to their feet. The clapping almost raised the roof and Ms Brannan had to shout to make herself heard as she darted out on to the stage.

CLAP
CLAP!!

"Right! Good! Now, on with the play!"

The audience's applause turned to boos and groans. "No, please. No more!"

"It was rubbish!"

"Way to go, Beaky!"

I couldn't see Madame Shirley now. I was about to hurl myself into the crowd when I felt Evie's hand slip into mine. "I think they want us to take a bow," she said. As we lowered our heads, everyone cheered and stamped their feet.

Then the cheering turned to laughter and I looked round to see Wayne stumbling out of the wings in the dog-suit. The head had been sewn back on along with a couple of alien-like tails, and the worst of the damage had been covered with shiny silver stars and moons.

"So ... what?" he demanded. "I got dressed up in this thing for nothing? *Again?*"

Over the laughter, I heard another sound. A deep, guttural growling that I recognized all too well.

The hall's main door stood open, revealing Destructo framed in the doorway. All the hair on the back of his neck was standing up and his eyes were locked on Wayne.

"How did he get out?" Mum yelped.

"My car!" said Dad, rushing towards the side exit. "I bet he's eaten the car!"

"N-no. Not again!" Wayne stammered, as Destructo tore towards the stage.

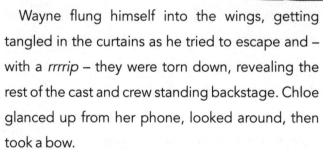

Wayne flung himself into the wings, getting tangled in the curtains as he tried to escape and – with a *rrrrip* – they were torn down, revealing the rest of the cast and crew standing backstage. Chloe glanced up from her phone, looked around, then took a bow.

Meanwhile Wayne let out a series of muffled screams as he stumbled out through a fire exit and ran off into the night.

After another burst of applause, the audience quickly began to file out in case Ms Brannan made us carry on with the play.

"Wait right there," I told Evie, then I jumped off the stage and shoved my way through the crowd, searching for Madame Shirley.

She couldn't have gone far. She had to be there somewhere.

I couldn't find her in the hall or out in the corridor or even in the school foyer. I hurried out into the cool evening air but all I saw were a few parents and kids headed for the car park.

I'd lost her. Again.

I was about to head back inside when something green and shiny fluttered past me on the breeze. It was an empty crisp packet.

An empty *pickled onion* crisp packet.

It looped in the air in front of me, then floated off to my right before banking sharply around the side of the school. Hurrying after it, I saw an old woman walking along the pavement just a few metres ahead.

It was Madame Shirley.

I'd finally found her!

"Wait!" I cried. "Madame Shirley! It's you, isn't it?"

The old woman turned round and waved at me.

"Hello, Beaky," she said. There was a rustling as she held a bag towards me. "Crisp?"

"What? Uh, no," I said. "Thanks."

Madame Shirley shrugged. "Suit yourself." She watched me for a moment then puffed out her cheeks. "Was there something you wanted to say to me?"

"Yes!" I said, still staring at her in disbelief.

"Well?" she chuckled. "What was it?"

I opened my mouth but nothing came out. What *did* I want to say to her? That she'd ruined my life? That I hated her for sticking me in that stupid machine? That she needed to put me back in and fix me?

I couldn't have said that stuff even if I'd wanted to. Because, well, it wasn't true. Not really. Not any more.

"Who *are* you?" I asked.

"I think you know who I am," she said, popping another crisp in her mouth and crunching it. "I'm Madame Shirley."

From the way she said it, I knew there was no point pressing the issue. She munched some more crisps, then smiled at me. "Was there anything else you wanted to say?"

"Uh ... yeah," I said. "Yeah. Um... Leon says 'thanks'."

"Does he? Wonderful!" Madame Shirley beamed. She tilted her head a little and looked me right in the eye. "And how about you, Beaky?"

"Um..." I thought for a moment, then said: "Let me get back to you on that."

Madame Shirley let out another little chuckle. "I'll look forward to it," she said, then she winked, turned away and strolled off along the pavement.

"There you are," said Evie, appearing beside me. "Who was the old lady?"

"Madame Shirley," I explained.

"She seemed … strange."

I smiled. "She is," I said. And then the moment was shattered by a costumed Wayne sprinting past us, screaming at the top of his lungs and trailing a stage curtain behind him. A few seconds later, Destructo almost knocked us over as he chased Wayne down.

Evie nodded. "I see what you mean. Your life *is* pretty complicated."

"Ain't that the truth," I said.

"There you are!" said Mum, as she, Dad, Jodie and Theo rounded the corner behind us. "We thought you'd eloped."

"I have no idea what that means," I admitted.

"Run off to get married," said Dad.

"God, no," Evie and I both said at the same time.

Jodie punched me on the arm. "That's for farting on my pillow," she said, then she shoved her hands in her pockets and marched ahead. "I'm going to meet Leon."

"What? Leon's here?" I said.

Jodie nodded. "He ran down to meet me. We're going to the cinema."

"He ran?" I said. "From *Aberdeen*?"

"Yep!"

I turned to Mum and Dad. "If you're worried about someone sneaking off to get married, you might want to catch up with Jodie."

My parents exchanged a worried glance, then set off at a rush. "Jodie! Not so fast..."

Theo, Evie and I stood together, like three points of a triangle. Theo puffed out his cheeks and looked at us both in turn. "So," he said. "What now?"

What now? It was a good question. For the first time in weeks, I was no longer obsessed with finding Madame Shirley. I was no longer the World's Greatest Liar, either, but maybe – just maybe – that wasn't such a bad thing.

"I don't know," I admitted. Then I smiled. "But we should probably start by saving Wayne."

Theo and Evie both gasped, then burst out laughing.

"Come on," I said, and the three of us ran off in pursuit of Destructo.

Together.

Read all the Beaky books!